TWO
of a
KIND
A Love Story

TWO of a KIND

A Love Story by Patrick Cauvin

Translated by Louise Barrett

DELACORTE PRESS/NEW YORK

Published by
Delacorte Press
1 Dag Hammarskjold Plaza
New York, N.Y. 10017

This work was first published in French by Editions Jean-Claude
Lattès as POURQUOI PAS NOUS? (© 1978, Editions
Jean-Claude Lattès).

English translation copyright © 1980 by Dell Publishing Co., Inc.

Manufactured in the United States of America

First printing

Designed by Terry Antonicelli

Library of Congress Cataloging in Publication Data

Cauvin, Patrick.
    Two of a kind.

    Translation of *Pourquoi pas nous?*
    I. Title.
PZ4.C3753Tw   [PQ2663.A847]   843'.914   80-10961
ISBN: 0-440-08670-1

TWO
of a
KIND

A Love Story

chapter one

THE vinyl freezes his buttocks through the maroon trunks.

I've never gotten used to it. What a body! I'm always surprised to be inside it.

The thigh muscles seem liquid, the masses of flesh rolling under Fredo's fingers like a sea. He lets his arms slide off the massage table and shakes loose the deltoids. It's harder and harder to loosen up the neck muscles before a fight. Tonight's gonna be a tough one.

"Three rounds and a knockdown . . ." the announcer bellows as Cro-Magnon comes in.

"The door, damn it!"

Cro-Magnon dives for the latch and the banging cuts off the voice of the speaker in the auditorium.

That's another strange thing: For twenty-three years every Saturday night he's felt like there's a cathedral on the other side of that wall. Something about the echo reverberating in the rafters and that wavering darkness in the rows of seats.

Fredo slaps his pectorals and it sounds like when the rue Ramey butcher lays the rump steak out on the stall to cut him a little pound-and-a-half slice. Directly in front of him, Cro-Magnon's dorsals are undulating. He adjusts the strap of his synthetic leopard bikini and takes his imitation sculptured flint cardboard club.

"You wanna go to Little Louis's tonight, Philippe?"

Philippe thinks how nice it'd be to finish off the evening with his pal. Little Louis always has a spicy stew that'll raise the dead. . . . It's calm; with the front grate closed they eat like real connoisseurs, very refined, with a little cold burgundy, just the way they like it. But, on the other hand, there is that geranium to finish.

"No, not tonight, pal, I'm working on my flowers."

It's incredible how hard it is to do a geranium. It's that velvety touch that's the worst, especially with watercolors. It's pure hell. First it shines, a beautiful lacquer; then, when it dries, it changes. Completely pockmarked. The guys who do oils have simplified their lives. One day I'll change to oils.

Cro-Magnon smiles, salutes with his club, opens the door, and wanders out reluctantly.

"Turn over, big boy."

Fredo chops his shoulder blades with the edge of his hand, and in the clouds of talc, Philippe sees the ash of his corn-paper Gitane in a close-up under Fredo's misshapen nose.

"You're gonna burn me with your cig."

Fredo lets loose a jet of smoke and massages the skin with his right hand while the left shakes the ash from the wet butt. The trainer chews his cigarettes as much as he smokes them. With a pinch on the rear, he signals that the session is over. Philippe Lipinchky gets down and stretches his 240 pounds.

Abdominal muscles ripple across his stomach, but on the upper thighs folds of fat are beginning to pad the bones. In spite of his six feet four inches, thickening has set in. *Careful, Philippe, six months and you'll have a spare tire.*

Thirty-seven and a half.

It's ridiculous: when asked his age, he always gives it in halves. Thirty-six and a half, thirty-seven and a half—like a little kid who wants to grow up faster. It makes his mother laugh.

Despite the walls, they hear the bellowing of the crowd explode above them.

Fredo smiles and millions of wrinkles cover his face.

"That's Léon going at it."

Léon is "Cro-Magnon." He plays the primate, hands dangling along the floor. He's a true comedian, Léon. He really makes you believe he's escaped from the Musée de l'Homme.

Philippe sits down in front of the broken mirror and takes his mask from the shelf. "He must have got his hold, the Neanderthal Lock. Can you tie my laces?"

He flattens out his hair, brushing back the curl so as not to have it in his eyes, and stretches the painted cloth. He pulls on his mask and adjusts it. Fredo tightens the strings behind his head.

"Loosen it up. This thing kills me."

"Shit! You're still not used to it?"

Philippe doesn't answer. The mask is red with black painted eyebrows starting at the top of his nose and spreading toward the temple like bat wings. A false mouth, open and grimacing, is painted on, with vampire teeth protruding over the lower lip.

"There you go, cute as can be."

Philippe stands in front of the mirror without really seeing his frightful image, wondering if what's missing in the nuance of those damned geraniums isn't a dot of straw yellow—something light, just the tip of the brush. And tomorrow I've got to see Maman in Courbevoie—no time to really get to work.

He gets up and opens his locker. Against the door, he contemplates his life-sized portrait; it's the poster of his tour in Quebec two years ago. Hands on hips; the mask, the red silk cape, and below, in flaming letters, his wrestling name: Mephisto King.

The guy who thought up that one was not dealing in nuance. *He* wouldn't have spent two weeks on a geranium petal. He's more likely a specialist in wall paint.

Philippe Lipinchky sighs, scratches his nose through the cloth, and turns around to greet Jean-François Bonsalvat, six foot seven, 270 pounds, who reaches out a hand that looks like a pound-and-a-half rib steak.

"How's it going, Philippe? I couldn't get here any sooner. My kid wanted me to help him with his stupid math problems."

He laughs. Philippe likes Bonsalvat; completely covered with blond fuzz, he's a big, smiling curly-headed boy—with an incredible punch. They've already been up against each other half a dozen times and understand each other like pros. Fredo saunters up.

"Want me to fix you up?"

Bonsalvat sits down on the massage table and dangles his feet in the air.

"Give me a cig instead and keep your pinkies to yourself. Philippe and me, we can raise the roof of the Palais des Sports with less effort than it takes to change the little guy's diapers."

Fredo shakes his head. Bonsalvat takes a drag off his Gauloise. On his back, across the mauve silk dressing gown, lined with gold lamé, is his name: *The Giant of the Abruzzes.*

He's got six kids, the Giant of the Abruzzes, and his wife runs a hatshop off the Place Clichy.

"Ready?"

The background noise continues.

"It's almost up, Léon's gonna take a dive in a minute. You two are up next."

Bonsalvat yawns.

"By the way," Philippe says dreamily, "where are the Abruzzes anyway?"

"Listen, pal, for me, beyond the strip between Clignancourt and Malakoff everything gets fuzzy. Oh yeah, be careful with my right knee, Bourassa just about exploded it last Saturday at Pantin. I was coming out of a left corkscrew and that jerk sweeps me into a scissor grip. He's a good guy, but he's not very careful."

Fredo nods his head.

Philippe slips on his cape. "Mephisto King," he says, "that's another thing I can't get used to. It's been three years now."

Bonsalvat laughs, takes one last drag, adjusts his protective cup, and gives his buddy a friendly tap on the shoulder.

"That's because you always get beat, but you're still the best mean guy around right now."

Philippe opens the door, followed by Fredo, and turns around.

"What'ya say we do twenty minutes? I'm not up to it tonight."

The vaulted walls go by, white tiles like in the underground passages of old train stations. It's the most decrepit room in the place. A real tunnel.

"Okay, I'll work out for eighteen minutes and flatten you in the twentieth."

The rumbling increases, echoing in the walls— the impression of coming out onto a subway platform.

Roars. The spotlights explode.

Eyelids blink under the brutal attack of the surrounding lights.

The roaring voices rise to the rafters, where the sounds merge with the metal framework, crash into the stained glass, then fall again as rain.

"And here he is . . . Mephisto King!"

Clanging of cymbals: *The Damnation of Faust.*

The manager's latest find; I come out in a satanic frenzy, the entire Philadelphia Orchestra behind me. A miracle of the tape recorder.

"Heavyweight combat between . . ."

The circus has begun. It's funny, really. The

music hall, theatrical effects . . . Sarah Bernhardt
. . . Mistinguett.

". . . two hundred thirty-eight pounds, ten
ounces . . . and the Giant of the Abruzzes . . ."

Philippe climbs through the ropes, kicks away a
Popsicle stick that has just landed on the mat, and
leans toward Fredo, who yells into his ear:

"Can you drop me at Barbès, if it's not out of
your way?"

Philippe nods and does a deep-knee bend. The
stagelights cut out a white triangle of bright light;
no shadows, a pure block.

Referee in the middle, black bow tie, immaculate
shirt front.

"Bastard! Bastard! Bastard!"

A woman is shouting from the balcony. She's
yelling at me, Philippe thinks. Maybe she's abused
so much that now all she can do is be abusive. . . .
A life with nothing but dishes, kids, public housing. . . . So Saturday night she comes to massacre
Mephisto. That's what we're here for.

It's our social function, an escape valve for those
overwhelmed by their existence.

Good God, philosophical wrestlers, that's really
something. . . .

"Just the hands, lay off the hair, show your soles.
How's your kid, Bonsalvat?"

Solid as a rock, the referee: Pedro Jouillat,
twenty-five years in the business, an old hand at
Greco-Roman; he knows us all. I'm beginning to
think we're just one big family.

From the corner of his mouth, pointing a warning finger, he gives a final admonition:

"The crowd's hot tonight, Mephisto, don't force it too much. Few weeks ago they broke up some benches."

Philippe gives a reassuring wink, takes his cape in his right fist, and sends it flying into the corner, where Fredo recovers it.

So, on with the one-man show.

With the slow step of a conqueror, flexing his pectorals, Mephisto King eyes the already raging crowd.

"Bastard! Bastard!"

The old biddy's completely crazed. No question, she's got it in for me.

At the sound of the bell Philippe pivots, gathers his strength, and forces himself into resembling a creature from Hell. He'll be at it for twenty minutes.

The same impressions, the same image; it's been my life for a long time now. It's my profession. . . .

Bonsalvat hops around, his face exposed, blond, bright, beautiful, and good.

Now for some cowardice!

Mephisto, impressed by the Giant's stance, retreats, raising a hypocritically appeasing hand, and backs into the ropes.

Bonsalvat approaches, looks disdainfully at the abject terror of his adversary, and turns around, disgusted.

A perfectly conceived number. Bonsalvat always has his back turned. Mephisto King shoots out and takes him in a headlock, which fells the Giant of the Abruzzes; indifferent to the frantic hopping about of the referee, he marches around victoriously, arms raised amongst flying peanut shells and rolled-up newspapers.

Booed by the furious crowd, Philippe Lipinchky, thirty-seven and a half, professional wrestler, bachelor, amateur painter, struts his 240 pounds of muscle around the ring, wondering if he might not bring out the background of his painting with a twilight of Prussian blue to accentuate the rosy warmth of the dying geraniums.

chapter two

It's Monday in Perpignan.

"Put me down for five Malrauxes and six complete Balzacs in paperback. They're selling quite well. And I'd also like . . ."

Jacqueline Puisset thinks it over. She pushes her tinted glasses up on her forehead, shuts her eyes, and rubs the bridge of her nose where the metal frames rest.

". . . from the Larousse collection I'll need *Cinna* and *Rodogune,* about thirty of each for the tenth graders."

Jacqueline Puisset looks up at the shelves of books surrounding her, and it's clear why she wears tinted glasses: she is walleyed. She's wondered for a long time if she wouldn't have preferred to be cross-eyed. Crossed eyes have a more concentrated effect, therefore more serious, therefore better for business. With the walleye it's more dreamy, more flighty. But really, neither's very attractive.

Jacqueline Puisset, bookseller, fingers the books

she's ordered, holding the telephone between her chin and collarbone.

"Wait, I need some Agatha Christies. Give me . . ."

Three customers come in. Jacqueline knows these three. They're real busybodies, but they do buy, and not just some little paperback, usually a big art book with glossy paper; but you have to look after them—otherwise they're like a tornado, Attila in the shelves. And Fabienne is at the discount shelf, behind the piles of Gallimards, redoing her makeup.

"I'll call you back for the orders, I've got lots of people in the store and . . ."

Outside, the sun is setting, golden on the pink flagstones. Peering through the window displays, Jacqueline notices the glowing softness of her street. It'll be that way for a while now; summer's hardly begun, and it lasts a long time here. She'll live the next few months behind the reddish-gold dew on the windows. Her favorite moment is in the morning when she opens the store: it's the last freshness before the heat of the long day. At the foot of the crosswalk she looks beyond the red tiles to the ribbon of sky stretched above her, knowing she's about to spend long hours inside the store. It's still dark and fresh like a forest. She looks over the new arrivals, thinking that books are like trees, full of leaves, and it feels good to be there. . . . Pretty soon the first customers come in; then Fabienne, late, out of breath, always with a different excuse . . .

"Do you need help?"

The three customers smile, all together.

"Hello, Mademoiselle Puisset. Don't trouble yourself, we're just looking."

Jacqueline turns away, back toward the counter, and in comes Trotsky, philosophy teacher at the high school. They call him Trotsky because he looks like Trotsky and he talks to his students about Trotsky.

His eyes sparkle with revolution under his Trotskyish spectacles.

"Did you receive my order, by any chance?"

Jacqueline dives under the counter and comes back victorious, holding a thin booklet of fifty pages, with a yellowed cover where climbing roses and clover interlace, in the style of the twenties. In the center a svelte lady is wrapped around a fountain. Title: *Exquisite Pallor,* by Noémie de Lavalande.

"Here it is, Monsieur Javier."

Always tempted to call him Trotsky, of course.

There's a kind of silent agreement between them, a secret pact: she speaks to no one about what he reads. If he were ordering pornographic books he wouldn't be more ashamed, but he knows he can count on her silence. He often comes in to chat with her. He tells her about his student's latest pranks. . . . He punishes them but it doesn't do any good. At home the tenant's six kids scream and play the guitar. He goes from one uproar to another, looking like the commander of the Red Army. Here, it's a kind of haven for him, a respite amongst the books. Many go to a bar, he comes to Puisset's . . . it's calmer.

Trotsky turns the pages slowly. At his fingertips everything becomes fragile. Books turn into porcelain in his hands.

"Noémie de Lavalande," he murmurs, "an exquisite woman. She must have spent her entire life glid-

ing through parks filled with angels on tombstones
silhouetted against the twilight. This kind of person
no longer exists."

Jacqueline smiles. When he gets going, there's no
stopping him. . . . I could listen to him for hours,
especially when he talks about the Romantics. He
knows Lamartine by heart; Musset's at the tip of
his fingers; Vigny from beginning to end . . .

Trotsky reads and exclaims:

"Listen to this, mademoiselle!"

He clears his throat, turns pink, and emotes:

"Diaphanous spells, scarlet autumns . . ."

He keeps time as if he were conducting the Phil-
harmonic.

"It's marvelous—there's an entire world ex-
pressed here, a universe of lace, castles in ruins,
sculptured foliage . . ."

Complete ecstasy. Trotsky is soaring; the Red
Army is far away.

"There's such charm in the words *diaphanous
spells*. Do you hear the music? Everything only a
turn-of-the-century vocabulary can suggest . . . the
softness of fading things."

He'll be at it for a while now.

Fabienne, back from the discount shelf, stations
herself behind him; she's clutching *The Life of Poulidor* and seems fascinated by the recital.

She looks at him as though *he* were Noémie de
Lavalande himself, with lace veil, teacup, powder
puff, fur muff, and tortoiseshell looking glass.

I've noticed that every time he starts one of his
tirades, she approaches and gapes in admiration
until her jaw drops.

"I wanted to ask you to order . . ."

He blushes as usual, hands Jacqueline a piece of paper, coughing.

"I wrote it out for you. It's easier, and I marked the publisher; it may well be out of print though."

He's scribbled: *Songs for Our Loves Gone By,* by Georgina Lancelot Mérédith.

"A true wonder, mademoiselle. This already quite old collection has several alexandrines that, in my opinion . . ."

"It's how much? *The Life of Poulidor?*" Fabienne interrupts timidly.

Trotsky looks at her as though she has just poured lentil soup on the whipped cream and faded-rose dresses of Noémie Georgina Lavalande Lancelot Mérédith.

"Forty francs," I tell her.

Trotsky stashes his purchases under his arm.

"I'm disturbing you, excuse me, but it is so pleasant to chat with you."

He doesn't hear my protests and has already fled down the aisle. I turn toward Fabienne to tell her off; after all, she could have waited a minute and not interrupted him; but, as usual, my courage fails me.

Fabienne is not Fabienne: she's Venus.

Fabienne Venus.

Bright-eyed, shining lips. I can't say anything to her, she's so beautiful. She's the one who made me realize that beauty is simply the fine line between too much and not enough. Balance, just enough, not more, not less. Me, I've got too much mouth, not enough nose . . . a disordered face . . . and then the eye, of course. What good can there possibly be in having a face like that? A childhood in tears, an adolescence of envy. . . . At forty I'm gradually starting to get used to it, and still, I . . .

"Hello, yes?"

"Jacqueline, it's Odette. Can you come by around five? Madame Munez is serving wine and would like it if . . ."

I'll have to go. But I don't like leaving the store. Plus, I've got to go by the notary's to see about the second floor; Fabienne will never be able to handle it.

"D'you have a book called *Rock and . . .*"

The boy unfolds a scrap of newspaper and attempts to decipher some penciled scribbling. ". . . *Rock, Grandeur and Decadence.*"

"Do you have the name of the publisher?"

"Uh . . . nope."

"Okay, Odette, I'll come by as soon as I can. Good-bye, Odette."

My life is filled up; not a minute to think about who I am. The store, the senior citizen's club, the library, the ciné club, my sister, my nephews, my brother-in-law, my project for the second floor. . . . Beautiful or ugly, it wouldn't make any difference.

"Fabienne, look on the music shelf, it's for the young man. A book about rock."

Fabienne arrives, revealing her beauty, eyelashes redone, thighs firm, turned-up nose. She's a walking temptation, this girl. The rocker is completely taken.

She does bring in customers, Fabienne, usually distinguished gentlemen, the type for a weekend in Collioure at a four-star hotel. She's the one they ask for the detective novels with naked women on the front, blondes on motorcycles camouflaged behind machine guns . . . it sells better than the feminist magazines.

"*Rock, Grandeur and Decadence:* twelve francs, seventy-five."

"How much?"

"Twelve francs, seventy-five."

"Oh! Uh . . . can you put it aside for me?"

He is completely scarlet, the poor thing. Even with Elvis Presley on his T-shirt he doesn't seem to have much confidence.

"Of course. You can come and pick it up whenever you like."

He sputters something and slithers out, ears on fire.

"Mademoiselle Puisset, are there any Médicis left?"

"On reserve, Fabienne. . . . Just a moment, ma'am, she'll get it for you."

Not a minute to do the bills, and I promised to call the distributor for the orders. And then there's François, who wants me to be on his list for the town council. He's no fool, my brother-in-law. He knows how to use the family, the beautiful one for love, the ugly one for politics.

I hated my sister for twenty years because her eyes went in the same direction.

"So, Fabienne, did you find the Médicis?"

"I've got it, mademoiselle."

Jacqueline smiles at the customer. "She'll bring it for you right away, ma'am."

When I smile like that I know I must look like a hatcheck girl waiting for her tip.

One time, I thought I would strangle my sister.

We had the same dress. Exactly. Mother insisted. At ten you think organdy and lace are going to straighten out your eyes. When I saw Noëlle the shock was too much. She was porcelain, Dresden china, pure joy emanating from her skin, beauty abounding. As for myself, I took a sideways glance at the mirrored wardrobe. I still don't know exactly why, but when I saw myself, I . . . well, it was appalling. Obviously the organdy had not transformed me; the contrast between the pretty dress and the rest was not exactly. . . . Anyway, it aggravated my ugliness. And Noëlle aggravated it too. Everything did. It was always there and always would be. I could try all the creams, permanents, different fabrics I liked, it would still be me underneath, until death, while Noëlle simply radiated without the slightest effort. We were quite a pair: day and night, the beauty and the beast. And the less she tried, the more she glowed, a disquieting splendor . . . so I let her have it. They had to separate us, and of course, I was the one who had to spend three days in my room, three days of tears, total depression. . . . I dreamt of operations, plastic surgery, going into department stores where they suggested various faces, masks that would never come off, that would become me. Then, she had her first flirtations, and each time she'd have a new one, I drenched my pillow. I fell apart, I cried so hard. There was no lull between the downpours; I was stepping over puddles—a life of tears and urges to strangle.

"Excuse me, the paperback Larousse, please . . ."

"The dictionaries are at the back of the store, on the shelf on the right. You can see it from here."

No boys for me, of course, they're no fools. No

big events in my life. So I finished high school at
fifteen; sure, there were certainly no romances taking up my time. Everyone liked me fine. That's the
worst. They'd never forget to invite me. Well, at
least they were charitable. In that respect, it was
better than childhood.

It's a charming period, childhood, everyone says
so: innocence, games, laughter . . . the times they
call you "eagle-eye," "walleye." I got out of it as
fast as I could. Deep down, I've always dreamt of
being sixty.

I can't get my orders filled. What am I doing
thinking about the past this morning . . . ?

"Mademoiselle Puisset, *A Pair of Rascals*—it's
in the Youth collection, isn't it?"

"No, the Golden Age. Fabienne, could you stay
alone for about an hour this afternoon?"

Panicked. The slightest thing can do it.

"Just an hour, then you can leave. I'll do the
arranging alone."

"Of course, Mademoiselle Jacqueline."

Barely eleven o'clock and . . .

Telephone. Well, it's my nearly strangled sister.

"You simply must come Saturday. I promise
François won't talk politics."

Jacqueline laughs.

"I'll come. How are things?"

"André's got the flu. He drinks gallons of syrup;
I have a feeling that's what makes him cough. He's
determined to be over it by his birthday. Can you
bring some books for Patrick? He *does* love to read."

"That's convenient."

The aunt. Well, it had to be, it was my fate:
hordes of little nephews. "Tata," that is, substitute

mother-aunt. I keep them supplied in adventure
stories, wipe their noses when Noëlle's worn out,
babysit so she and François can go out. Eventually
I'll sign their report cards. I was made to be a bookseller and aunt. So why am I complaining?

". . . we can't all fit in the car anyway, so . . ."

Jacqueline is no longer listening. The store is
packed right now. They're from the Our Lady of
the Blessed Sacrament school and have come for
Pascal's *Pensées*. The boarders are squirming in their
grayish ankle socks and princess hats.

"Fabienne!"

She's gone, Marilyn Monroe. It's unbelievable to
be so beautiful—and more unbelievable to work so
hard at it.

I'm the one who ought to spend the day with
mascaras and what-d'you-call-its. That would be
understandable. But her. . . . Beauty must be like
money: the more you've got, the more you want.
The Beauty of Perpignan graces the surroundings
with her countenance, three-fourths velvet, one-
fourth emerald.

In fact, I wonder what she's doing in a bookstore;
if I were she, I'd . . . I don't know . . . Miss World,
movie star, secret agent, cover girl. It's ridiculous,
really, enveloped in this sumptuous gift she doesn't
know what to do with. It bothers me that she's not
happier. This girl has everything . . . everything I'd
want, that is, everything I would have wanted.

Here are the other three back with a history of
Italian painting for 180 francs. . . . I don't have
time to chat with them. . . . The phone. My empty
life is completely packed.

A hopeful young man, no doubt.

"Hello. Yes, Marguerite . . . I'll come by and see you. No, it's not difficult. . . . I'll come as quickly as possible . . . but right now. . . . Fine, very good. Bye, Marguerite."

Marguerite's bills—fifteen years I've been typing them. I don't know how I'm going to do it all when I open the reading room upstairs. I'll have to have a girl to keep an eye on things, or rather, to give advice, to read aloud. Not Fabienne, she'd be too sexy for them. And I'll need some armchairs for the old ladies. . . . How do I get myself into these things?!

I know what you're giggling about, you two behind the postcards. I'm so used to it I'm beginning to not give a damn.

"Can I help you, young ladies?"

Seeing me up close, that cuts the laughter.

"Two ball-point pens at three francs, twenty; an eraser at one franc, forty . . . that'll be seven francs, eighty . . ."

Fabienne rings up the Pascal's *Pensées*.

The sun is at its height. In a few hours blue shadows will invade the bookstore, from the bestsellers to the cheap paperbacks. . . . Literature does not escape the night.

The customers thumb through books.

Bbrrring!

Jacqueline Puisset picks up the phone, thinking how silly it is to believe that life could have been different, when it's not all that bad the way it is.

chapter three

TEN past midnight.

All is quiet in the little house, one of many set on the northeastern slope of Montmartre.

Alone on the top floor, in his "two rooms and a kitchen," Philippe Lipinchky is still up.

Hair plastered down from his shower, he collapses on the sofa, Aunt Lucienne's sofa, with the two arm-protectors representing the Circus of Gavarnie and the Rock of Rocamadour.

He dropped Fredo off at the metal grill of the métro entrance and miraculously found a place at the bottom of the hill, right between the mechanic's tow truck and a van.

Now, in the midst of red-chalk sketches and portfolios, his geraniums are waiting. Philippe looks them over with a doubtful eye. It's true, they do look strange, as though maybe they faded during the match. In any case they don't look much like geraniums.

Philippe sighs, walks over to the fridge, and takes out an entire ham, a head of romaine, and a carton of eggs.

The night is infinitely calm. He walks in stocking feet, careful not to make the floor squeak because of Mme. Vignoux and her insomnia. The slightest noise wakes her up.

"I just don't sleep, my boy . . . less and less . . ."

Seventy-seven this summer, Mme. Vignoux. He's known her for years.

The six eggs glisten in the pan, bubbles rising imperceptibly from the simmering butter.

A dash of tarragon vinegar. The whites are already firm.

A perfect match. Bonsalvat's really a good guy. One of these days he'll have to accept Bonsalvat's invitation, even though he doesn't like to go out much. Either he holds back or else he eats his fill, and then he's not invited back.

With Léon it's different. He's a friend.

Now and then when they fight each other, they really go at it for a couple of minutes. A body slam followed by a cradle. . . . The last time, at Alfortville, it was a pile driver and then into an armlock.

That's when I realized I still have the punch. Seventeen years on the mat and still a little voltage in the old backbreaker. Makes me feel good to think about it. Where did I put the wild thyme?

The oil shines in the crevices of the lettuce. . . . I love fixing my dinner. Seventeen years on the mat and thirty-seven as a bachelor. Good training for a cook.

The steel blade chops through the chives. There's

just one guy who sells them fresh, in a wooden cart
on rue Lepic; a retired boxer, used to be at Breton-
nel's, a featherweight from the thirties.
Do I fry up some bacon or let it go?
Let it go.
A carafe of icy rosé to oil the pipes and the feast
is on.
Tiptoeing over, delicate as a ballerina, Philippe
Lipinchky, connoisseur, sits down to his meal, whets
his appetite with two lettuce leaves, adds three grains
of salt to the dressing, and unfolds his napkin.
He chews slowly. Outside, beyond his windows
opening out onto the roofs, Paris calms down,
drowned in moonlight, a floating body in the night.
The windowpanes reflect the impressive size of
this human colossus and his strangely sculptured
face.
"You know what we really look like, the two of
us?" Léon had said. "A pair of boiled potatoes."
That wasn't so long ago, five years maybe; but in
fact, it'd always been that way. Even when he was
fifteen, he already looked like a damned potato. You
could see it in the snapshots—the vacation at Arcachon when he was fourteen and already at 170
pounds. Even with his tight clothes it was obvious
he was built like a tank, muscles busting out everywhere. He'd shed enough tears over it—those tri-
ceps, those quadriceps, that huge growing mountain
that was himself. At the beach those minute, grace-
ful girls running around, with curved waists and
arms like glass. He'd only had distant, breakable
loves. In his dreams he was always small and
slender.

"It's his father. . . ."

Two hundred ninety pounds, Papa, and a weight lifter to boot, king of the clean and jerk, who loved to knock back shots of "dry white." Could down seven liters in twenty-four hours. Cirrhosis of the liver plus barbells: ideal for being fatherless at age eleven. Eleven and a half.

The best ham in Paris; there, too, you have to know about it . . . not let them pass that stuff in cellophane off on you.

With the first egg fried almost to the burning point, a chunk of cold meat provides exactly the contrast he's after.

Young girls pass through his memory. No boy ever saw so many girls go by . . . in August on the beaches of Arcachon . . . in the streets of Courbevoie where they lived. There was a high school right across the street; rosy-cheeked nymphettes, squeals of laughter spinning the weathervane on the old church, and him in the midst of it all, already at 175 pounds, with hands like a strangler's, a nightmare on "weighing and measuring" day.

Maybe now they'd like it, it might be attractive, but at the time muscle was not an advantage, the fashion was not the brick-wall build. Oh well, that's how you blow the love of your life. . . .

The cold wine stings his tongue. Halfway through the meal he grants himself a filtered Gauloise: the second and last of the day. It's weird to be thinking about all that tonight. . . . Mephisto and his fried eggs. There was one girl he traveled around with; they rambled together along sunny shores, in the hearts of dead cities, on scarlet terraces, in sleds along snowy forest trails, on tropical beaches. She wore a beret and bought her wine from the barrel, ten degrees, at the grocery on avenue Gambetta. No girl ever traveled so much without knowing it. . . .

He smashes his butt in the Dubonnet ashtray he stole from Little Louis's and swallows the last two eggs in one bite.

Then one day, rainier than most, a day when he was hanging out between the train-track passageway and the towing path, he had run up and rushed into the gym; the guy had asked him:

"How old are you?"

"Fifteen."

He sniffed a little harder.

"Boxing?"

"No . . . I . . . I'd rather wrestle."

So it all started. Right away, he knew he'd found it. There was the smell, the tiles, the cold water, the incredible efforts, just about busting the veins when they picked each other up, the full-arm lifts he can't do anymore.

And the years passed . . . Mephisto. . . . Wrestling paid all right, and there was the spectacle of it, amateur champion of France, the matches on TV. He was a big guy among others; he lived with them and felt good there. Sometimes there were surly ones, pea-brained guys who liked the rough stuff, but no more than anywhere else. In his neighborhood no one knew he was Mephisto; there was just the man in the cheese shop who had discovered it, in spite of the mask. He's a little guy, the cheese man: barely five feet on tiptoes, but what an imitation of a Japanese overhead throw! He makes the

Swiss cheese dance with that one. One day he mysteriously led Philippe to the back room, which was soaked in the aroma of Roquefort.

"Monsieur Philippe, could it be you, Mephisto King?"

He hadn't denied it. The cheese man had the eye; he had recognized his shoulder span in the poster.

"If you don't mind, I'd rather you not tell anyone. You know how people are—they might think I'm the same in real life as in the ring."

The cheese man had sworn:

"I won't tell anyone, Monsieur Mephisto, not even my wife. I'm gonna go see you Saturday at Wagram. Have you tried my *gaperon* with garlic? It's my treat."

He's the one who taught Philippe how to make cheese cocktails.

Philippe gets up and opens the outdoor cupboard. He takes a cloth-covered board and puts it gently on the table. Underneath, there's a crust of Chavignol, a little Brie, some mimolette, a triangle of Muenster, some bleu d'Auvergne, and a piece of Avesnes hardly even touched.

Starting with Camembert, he adds a noisette of butter, gives it body with some Muenster, perfumes with chèvre, mixes thoroughly with a fork, then splashes on a three-star cognac. Once he's worked up a smooth paste, he spreads it half the length of a long piece of bread and digs into a royal treat.

His nostrils savor the combined aroma of the tangled flavors. He chews slowly, sighing with contentment. His eye wanders toward his watercolors.

In a few minutes he'll get started. He loves this moment just before, the instant when he senses the long hours lying before him in the company of his tubes, paper, and brushes.

The wind circling the Sacré-Coeur gently pushes the half-opened window, and Philippe sees himself reflected in the pane.

A big guy with the face of a gentle brute gulping down a gigantic roll spread with cheese, lazing around nice and cozy in his little apartment. Getting a little gray around the temples, but this front lock has a nice curl to it. A curly lock like Clark Gable's. Too bad it's only the lock.

He winks at his reflection, thinking that tonight there are two things that are sure. First, that he is not unhappy, and second, that he is not happy either.

He washes his hands, using a trickle of water so as not to make the pipes creak and wake up Mme. Vignoux, and begins his artistic vigil.

He won't be in bed until dawn, the hour of the first cyclists, when the black of night turns a mousy gray, and the rumble of the first métros rises from the bowels of the city.

chapter four

THROUGH the sparkling yellow bubbles of the mousseux, Mme. Munez's face takes on the elongated shape of the champagne glass.

"To your health, Mademoiselle Puisset!"

She always feels good with them. For as long as she can remember, she's never been bored in their company.

Maybe it's because they are beyond beauty and its opposite. All that is no longer important; they are beyond category, almost beyond life. Maybe that's why they always seem to be laughing too.

Everyone clinks glasses. They've put on their russet lace collars; their skirts are more carefully pressed today.

It's the senior citizen's club. She'd had the idea to set up this reading room, and brings the books and magazines they like. She comes whenever she can.

The old men continue playing cards. They don't

mix too much with the women. Theirs is a genera-
tion unfamiliar with mixed socializing . . . as though
today it's any different.

"To your youth, Madame Munez!"

They all laugh. It doesn't take much—less and
less really—a little ham, a few crackers, a little
sleep, laughter. Odette passes around the cookies,
the birthday cookies that crumble into dust and stick
like the Sahara in your esophagus. For the most
part, they love them.

I'll be like that one day. Then it'll no longer be
the time of possible loves but the time of past loves,
and all I'll have to do is invent mine.

"I prefer the last one because I like books where
you see people age, where you follow an entire life,
and then you see the outfits in the beginning, with
the hoop skirts and pleated pants, and at the end
it's almost like nowadays."

Mme. Nalard, with her coat still on so no one
will miss the fur collar, leans over:

"It's true, and the interiors are described so well!
The servants, the lace doilies; it makes me think of
the ones I had before my beloved passed on—all of
them crocheted. What patience that takes! Plus, I
like it when there's emotion like that."

The other sets down her glass and moves closer.

"And you, Mademoiselle Puisset, since you have
the bookstore, you don't perhaps know if there'll be
a sequel, do you?"

Jacqueline smiles, half-choking on her chalky
cookie.

"It's hard to say, but I imagine if the book is a
success . . ."

Mme. Nalard raises her hands as though a Colt

.45 had just been pointed between her shoulder blades. "I can assure you there will be; it's such a good story. You might say those are the kind of people you just don't meet every day in real life. The world just isn't like that anymore, and it's too bad too."

"Let's have some music, Madame Rossi."

Mme. Rossi bends over the record player. She's the one in charge: the only one who touches the equipment. It's a waltz; just a few notes, and ten Viennas and thirty Danubes emerge.

"It's nice of you to come, Mademoiselle Puisset."

I see my distant reflection in the windows giving out onto the courtyard and the plane trees. The silhouette isn't bad; it's reassuring to know that from a distance you're like other people. You can hardly tell I'll soon be getting fat. That'll really top it off: ten pounds more and there'll be no question I've given up the ghost, as though I hadn't already.

Pseudo-waltz and pseudo-champagne. Only the oldies are real. It's always the same, one glass and out come the emotions: forty years old and never been kissed. What good is it to have lips?

"Mademoiselle Puisset, we were wondering if you could come with us to Palavas."

"If I can . . . I'd love to. I'll let you know."

Oh God, the beach with a great horde of old ladies. . . . You have to cut up the sandwiches. They make police hats out of newspapers, are constantly looking for shade. Ten feet away couples are clinging in the dunes, tanned, silky, splendid. Then you have to gather up the herd: "It's five o'clock, ladies." No, I've done it a hundred times and I just can't. It's bad enough with Noëlle's kids—I guard the shovels and buckets. "Throw me the ball, Tata!" All those men passing by, men who might stop were my traveling eye not wandering toward the cumulus clouds. It's practical in a way, one eye on the nephews, the other on the sea gulls. Go ahead, joke around, Jacqueline, have another glass. I don't know why I'm not an alcoholic—lack of imagination, I guess.

What's wrong with me? It must be the music, their murderous cookies, the crummy wine, the heat. I haven't been this way for years. But I've got my life now, and it's full of things and people.

Jacqueline Puisset suddenly leaps up. The flaps of her dress fly out.

"Give me the tray, Odette. You just relax, I'll pass it around. Madame Munez, would you like a cookie?"

The old men smile at her as she approaches; they like her because she doesn't call them "Paps" or use language that's too familiar. It's unusual for them to be called by their names. Aging often means losing one's identity. What makes one old guy different from another? Wrinkles bring on uniformity.

They look at her hesitantly, not knowing quite where to focus. Which is the good eye?

"Come on, Mademoiselle Jacqueline, how about a dance?"

That's Vallier, seventy-eight springs next fall, and that's their waltz, which they've already played several times. . . . Same thing every time she comes.

"I don't have time, Monsieur Vallier, it's six o'clock and . . ."

"You can't do that to me, Mademoiselle Jacqueline, you just can't."

He's kidding, but what's lurking behind those looks? I know only too well what there is behind mine.

She puts down her empty glass and reaches out; the old man with the white porcelain dentures squeezes her waist in his trembling hands.

All right, let's go, my ancient lover. Who said I couldn't be coaxed to dance? Who said I never waltzed, my handsome, tender prince of love? You are lighter than air, so handsome, so gentle; look, I just need three glasses of bubbly and everything becomes intimate. . . . We glide over the snowy bridges of a deserted city; night has fallen, red with torches, gardens bustling with parties. I am as beautiful as you are young. They're all looking at us in silence. The archduke in his box seat. . . . How blond she is, Madame Munez, so slender and dazzling! The silk dresses, the jewels, the brightly made-up faces glowing under the chandeliers. Tomorrow we'll take the forest road, in sleds covered with furs, in the white silence of sleigh bells, kisses in the snow . . .

"Do you want to sit down, Mademoiselle Puisset?"

"No, Odette, it's okay."

Old Vallier is there looking at her, along with the others.

"It's the wine, I had a little too much . . . plus a little fatigue. I'm all right now."

She laughs first and the others follow.

"I've got to go. Please continue."

A grandmother with a Claudine collar, cotton stockings, and a yellow chignon whispers softly:

"I know what it's like, dear, I kept a business for fifty-three years. . . ."

Jacqueline shakes several hands, nods her head; everything wavers a bit but it's not unpleasant, like a barge floating on still water. . . . It's ridiculous to get drunk at a senior citizen's club. Come on, stop regretting things.

Odette accompanies her to the stairway.

"If you *could* go to Palavas, I know they'd appreciate it."

The sun is scorching, and it's late too. I'd like to be home, in the shade—a shower, brush my teeth to get rid of this terrible sweet taste, take three aspirins.

"I'll call you during the week, Odette."

My car. Another protection. Walls of sheet iron and glass. I like to own things, because they're mine, just as though I were pretty. No doubt about it, I had one glass too many.

The streets file by. It's an outer neighborhood she doesn't know too well, with a lot of recent construction—cement so white it hurts your eyes. There aren't enough flowers around here. Jacqueline drives slowly down the streets lined with children playing. A little girl on roller skates keeps up with her for a long time, a carefree race that makes her pigtails fly out.

Jacqueline takes a roundabout route to the center of the city. She's happy to feel the walls closing in, accumulating behind her: the enemy will not pass.

The high school. The old playground where I was haunted by Picture Day.

"Not so much profile, mademoiselle."

Sure, I walked away with all the awards, and Odette had to repeat the year, but she couldn't have cared less, she was the prettiest. It's funny how with problems in education they claim to ignore one's physical aspect, as if all students were equal. Josiane with her doe eyes could get away with anything, forgotten notebooks, unlearned lessons; all you need's a becoming tear, some aesthetic despair, and it all works out.

Right at the angle of the rue Gambetta is an enormous billboard. Girls prance about, showing off their panty hose—five feet ten, slinky and teasing, life is easy—a pair of panty hose and you're beautiful; a hair curler and happiness is yours. Beauty everywhere, as if perfection were normal, as if, in the kitchens of this town, at this moment before dinner, only Marilyn Monroes were slicing the tomatoes for the evening salads.

Jacqueline moves into the left lane. Through the lowered window comes a sea breeze that must have been whirling around the hills for it to smell so much like the golden reeds there.

I live in a world where fashion models rule: youth and charm, white teeth and shiny hair; they never shut up about it. I've got shiny hair too, for all the good it does me.

Here's the esplanade; this is my town, the long walkways lined with plane trees. I played hopscotch here, made castles in these sandboxes, and now I'm circling around in a Simca. That's progress. I will never drink mousseux again . . . and I don't think I'll eat tonight. It'll be nice to go to sleep with the window open wide, letting the night come in gently with the murmur of the town, the music of the TVs.

I'll do the bills tomorrow. I deserve a few lazy hours, a few hours of springtime spent just the way I like: eyelids shut.

Along the river, shutters are already closing out the night. This is the provinces; in a few minutes this entire area will be dead. The streets here are hardly big enough to be called streets; in general, life seems somewhat smothered. I've thought about leaving; if I'd been pretty I might have done it, but I would have missed the sunlit walls struck by the wind. I don't know, rue Mailly, rue de la Fusterie, rue des Théâtres—these little streets like knife marks separating the golden crust of the roofs. My town is a cake . . . a cake that I like.

A parking place. That's a minor miracle.

Jacqueline maneuvers the car into the place along the curb. The sidewalk still glistens from the water thrown by the café waiter pulling down the iron grate.

"You're lucky to find a place tonight."

Jacqueline turns around.

Leaning out on her flower-filled balcony, Mme. Cormosier smiles at the bookseller, her hands trembling. She's eighty-two, Mme. Cormosier; Jacqueline has known her for years. Behind the old lady enveloped in successive shawls and layered woolens, in the middle of summer, is her high-ceilinged living room, partially visible.

"You should come to the senior citizen's club, Madame Cormosier, it would be company for you."

The old lady shakes her head.

"I like it too much at home, Jacqueline."

It's nice when the old ladies in the windows know your first name.

She is surrounded by reflections of polished antique furniture on marble, old photographs. That, too, is the provinces, and Jacqueline hopes she'll always find that old wrinkled face smiling down at her for the rest of her life. You must be eternal, Madame Cormoisier; it'd be too painful for me if one day your shutters closed out the world.

Jacqueline walks on. In the narrow streets bordering the Castillet people are leaving the terraces as dinnertime smells rise with the first stars.

chapter five

SHE sits down under the rows of paintings circling the dining room and takes a sip of sweet wine.

"Do you need any help?"

"It'll be ready in three minutes."

At seventy-three, she doesn't look a day over seventy-two, as she likes to say. Even less on Sunday, when she primps a little for his visit.

Through the partly opened door she can see him buzzing around the kitchen. He does everything, always has—no question of her sticking her nose in there. Anyway, it's true she can hardly boil water.

He comes at nine o'clock on the dot with two baskets of fresh vegetables, cheeses, butter, an entire ham, and settles into the kitchen. It's his specialty. Two and half hours later, the *tarte aux épinards* comes out of the oven, the roast and vegetables are ready. She sets the table, serves the cocktails, and they eat, tête-à-tête, until one o'clock. Two hundred forty minutes of nonstop pestering.

An old ritual.

He arrives with the *tarte* and hands her the knife. "Your turn to serve."

With a sigh of satisfaction he looks at the water-colors clustered in rows. The shadows around the violets are beautiful; he painted them last year and had a terrible time keeping it neat, not too busy.

"Next time I'll bring you the geraniums."

Victoria Lipinchky sighs.

"With this heating through the floor, a flower can't possibly survive here."

Philippe swallows his aperitif and makes a face—sickeningly sweet. They must make this concoction out of old rubber tubes.

"They're not real ones; it's a watercolor."

Victoria glances doubtfully at her crowded walls.

"I hardly have any room left."

Philippe shrugs his shoulders.

"You can squeeze it in."

She knows there is nothing to say and says nothing. Before, when there was something to say, she still said nothing—an old habit acquired through years of factory life—garment worker, Buisson and Company, Levallois.

The only one she has never talked to about it is Philippe: she would have liked him to be a lawyer and defend the innocent, like in the movies. She had it all worked out: the guy practically condemned to death, bewildered, vacant, his head already in the guillotine; the jury packing up to go; and her son arrives with his counsel's speech. For two hours he pleads the man's cause as eyes begin to water, the public wavers, the bastard of a prosecutor slowly turns green; then, the verdict: not guilty. Philippe

collapses in a faint, totally exhausted, his curly lock
flung back. She rushes up with flowers—real ones,
not painted—and they leave with a standing ovation
in the courtroom. Instead of that, instead of the
beautiful black robe, he clowns it up in a ring, practically naked. . . . "They can't see me, I wear a
mask." Wonderful. That just shows that deep down,
he is ashamed.

And then, as if that weren't enough, he always
loses. That's the worst part. He's explained it to her
a thousand times, but she can't accept it.

"Did you play the bad guy again last night?"

Philippe nods with his mouth full. His mother
shakes her head.

"Why don't you change around with your friends?
You could be the good guy for once. It's only fair
that everyone get his turn to fall on the ground."

Philippe shakes his head. When she talks to him
about his work, he always answers with his head.

"I think it's better than last time."

It is really good, his *tarte*. Oh, what a good boy!
Strong and everything, even knows how to cook. I
know he doesn't like this, but I've got to get it out.

"So, you still haven't found a young lady?"

Philippe doesn't budge. It's a well-known song.

"I haven't had time to look this week."

Of course, he's not very, very handsome, but
beauty isn't everything.

"Philippe, beauty isn't everything. I've told you
that a hundred times."

"A hundred eighty."

"It's not a joke. One day you'll be old and all
alone. I'm not eternal, you know."

"I'm not so sure about that."

She finishes sipping her aperitif and points at him accusingly.

"It's not a joke. You have a few more years in front of you and then what are you going to do?"

"I have my savings account."

"Don't be ridiculous; with what you spend just on food, you won't last a year."

Philippe gets up.

"I'll get the roast."

She watches him walk out, grazing the door frame with his shoulders. She hears him rummage through the kitchen drawer.

"Don't worry about it. I'll open a new ring with Léon and some of the guys. I'll get by."

"You always say you'll get by."

He comes back with the roast, a golden brown, crowned with green beans and matchstick potatoes. His smile is back.

"So, I don't get by all right?"

When he smiles like that he's even uglier, my little boy, my colossal little boy. I've seen girls looking at you . . . the little bitches, I could have killed them. But sure, go ahead, it's true you'll get by, you'll do okay. Me too, I came through it . . . in pieces.

I run around, scold you, aggravate you with my questions about this fiancée who never comes, but it's because ever since you were born, I've wanted to not have to beg your pardon. For thirty years now I've resisted the desire. I'm an old woman, a little tough, a little grumpy, and I'm sure it seems like I've been bugging you constantly, but that's because I've never stopped feeling guilty. Something in me, in my body, has made you ugly, Philippe.

I don't understand it, I never will. Your father had your build but not your face; I think you could say he was handsome . . . my handsome drunkard.

I followed the blooming of this ugliness, which followed you from the cradle to your first day of school. This is my work; I caused it and I don't understand.

I was not a very sweet mother, Philippe, but you can't reproach me with having seen me cry. I hid myself too well for that; I couldn't have told you the reason for my tears.

How I would have liked for you to suffer less than I did. Waiting at the school on rue Roussel for that explosion of pretty little children with dimples and soft cheeks, I'd lean against the wall to keep from dying. Surrounded by women whose bodies had not betrayed them. And there you were with your book-bag, my sweet, clumsy little oaf.

If I didn't lean down to kiss you. Philippe, it's because all the seas and oceans were welling up in my eyes and might have poured out. I was like a pitcher those days, tilt me and I cried. I'd walk away, my head stiff, and you'd trot behind me, probably thinking I didn't love you. Even today, I know you think I'm a hard woman. I say what I think. I'm a little too abrupt and not too clever. It's just that I've never stopped begging your pardon and I don't want you to notice. . . .

"Shall I serve you?"

She holds out her plate. Thirty yards below them, the exit ramp from the Paris–Pontoise freeway is still fairly calm. From five o'clock on it's really going strong; up until midnight it's the weekend crowd coming back. I'm lucky to be on the twelfth floor, the noise is muffled a little. We had a house before they tore down the neighborhood. I'm not complaining, I've got an elevator and a garbage chute. Plus Philippe comes so often! We call each other. . . . He insisted I get a phone.

"You still haven't bought a TV, Philippe?"

"No."

She sighs again. He knows it's completely useless, but he explains anyway:

"I'm on the road so much, plus I've got my painting, or else I read."

"That doesn't keep you from having one."

Madame Mephisto. That's what he called her the other day. Fortunately no one knows—it'd make quite a hit with the concierge! "Your mail, Madame Mephisto. So, was he thrown again, your little boy? That'll teach him to be so devilish."

Philippe finishes off the *mareuil* and washes it down with an old Bordeaux. He got off easier than usual this time. Could mean she's more worried than usual.

"I've got about five more years. After that I'll give it up and start training the young ones. I've told you not to worry, there's plenty of demand."

He puts his first Gauloise of the day in the corner of his mouth and lights a match, causing every muscle in his forearm to undulate up to the elbow.

Just like his father.

The clock in the bedroom strikes one, the time when normal people sit down to eat. They've already finished. Philippe wrestles at five o'clock and needs the time to digest.

"Where are you going today?"

"Saint-Ouen. Two rounds, maybe a runoff."

"Are you going to lose again?"

He nods. He's going to get thrown by Roger Dumonchel, the Angel of Haut-de-Seine: with chronic bronchitis and muscles like marshmallows, he could get flattened by a breeze.

Telephone.

Victoria Lipinchky majestically picks up the receiver as though she were the Empress of Russia.

"Helloooo . . ."

She stands dreamily for a moment like an actress she's seen in a Sunday matinee, then hands the receiver over the table.

"It's for you."

Philippe listens, smiles, gathers crumbs with his index finger, emits three "okays," one "so long," and hangs up.

"A tour. Toulouse, Montpellier, and Perpignan, three days at the end of the week."

Victoria sighs.

"Well, at least you see the country a bit."

"What do you expect? It's not so bad to be able to say you're part of the jet set."

"That's it, rub it in."

Philippe smiles. Through half-closed eyes he surveys the aging lady opening the cardboard box. This time, like every time, the miracle occurs: In the creams and caramels climbing the Saint-Honoré pastry, Victoria Lipinchky rediscovers the delightful excitement of her childhood, and the wrestler's soul is filled with a sweet sadness.

At the windows of the public high-rise, the first

sparrows of summer burn their feet on the narrow iron balconies. The weather is already beautiful. Philippe leans back in the shadow of the curtain as the sunrays flood the painted flowers, pale-stemmed blossoms in watercolors.

It is one o'clock in Courbevoie.

chapter six

IT's over now, I can go to Noëlle's without fear. There was a time when it was horrible: she had it in her mind to fix me up, to somehow, somewhere, find me a husband or a lover. She meant well.

Any old lecherous bureaucrat or confused little jerk would be brought before her famous baked rabbit with olives. Obviously it was unplanned, very impromptu. "My sister, Jacqueline . . . Monsieur Vention, a colleague of François's." I've seen tons of them. Three fourths leave before finishing dessert. Always plenty of homemade pie left over. She must have told them I was no beauty, but they certainly weren't expecting that. It's too much for them. There was one who was vaguely attached; he called a few times. He had two characteristics: acute hemorrhoids and a desire to be a bookseller. I had to threaten Noëlle and François that I would never darken their door again. They promised to give it up.

Now I'm off with books for Patrick, felt-tip markers for Sebastian, and balls of wool for André's future sweater. If there's a present for one, then it's presents for all three—obviously it simplifies things. Then you add the weekly pizza in the pink cardboard box from my delicatessen (the best in the neighborhood) and a few other little goodies for my sister. . . .

I ring the doorbell, and panic breaks out.

"Tata! It's Tata!"

Kisses, more kisses; I get a few runny noses wiped on me. Patrick jumps on my back, revving up like the concierge's son's Yamaha. Noëlle yells from the kitchen:

"Have a seat in the living room. I'll be right there."

The three kids drag me off and open the door; the balls of wool roll away, the pizza almost follows, and what do I see in the living room? My brother-in-law standing up, straightening his tie, and turning toward the seat of honor.

"Jacqueline, I'd like you to meet Anselme Bertouin, a young colleague who . . ."

"Goddamnit."

I am a polite person, I have my master's in literature, run a good bookstore, but I said "Goddamnit."

Jacqueline disengages the last nephew from her shoulders, attempts a quarter-smile, shakes Anselme Bertouin's dead-fish hand, dumps the wool, pizza, and diverse packages into the armchair, and heads for the kitchen.

"Excuse me, I must tell Noëlle something."

The two men sit there, vaguely disconcerted, as Jacqueline bursts into the kitchen like a lunar missile.

Noëlle throws up her hands, knocking over the olive jar.

"It wasn't me," she whispers. "I swear to you it wasn't me, I didn't do anything."

Jacqueline Puisset grabs the wooden mallet and starts hammering the rabbit meat.

"How many times do I have to tell you to mind your own business! Who is this goon your husband's set aside for me?"

Noëlle puts her finger to her lips.

"He didn't really mean to, he just . . ."

"Listen, please don't lie about it as well. You know perfectly well that when François brings home a colleague, it's with the specific intention of transforming my existence overnight."

"No, not tonight, it was just to . . ."

"And what's more, if he's set him aside for me, there must be something wrong with him. What is it this time? A manic-depressive? A delirious maniac? Maybe another hemorrhoid sufferer?"

Noëlle plunges into the sauce as François appears and whispers violently:

"Are you coming out or not? I've had it, I don't know what to say to him."

Jacqueline laughs, pops an olive, and spits out the pit.

"You were counting on me to make conversation?"

Noëlle turns toward her husband.

"She thinks you invited him on account of her."

Suspiciously indignant, François looks at Jacqueline.

"Are you crazy? I've got better things to do than to constantly furnish men for you."

Really charming, my brother-in-law. I love the way he can be completely ridiculous without the slightest complex.

A variety of noises seeps in from the living room: Sebastian is yelling, the other two join in, and in the background is a kind of pitiful wailing, undoubtedly from Anselme.

François stamps his feet.

"All right, let's go, damn it. Hurry up, we're not going to leave him alone in there with the kids."

Surrounded and under siege, Anselme Bertouin seems happy to see us come back.

We all sit down.

It's incredible, the noise he can make chewing peanuts. You'd think it was a combine harvester.

Sebastian peers over his coloring book.

"Why do you make so much noise when you eat?"

The perfect hostess, Noëlle rushes to the victim's rescue.

"They are hard, aren't they? I opened the pack the day before yesterday and . . ."

I'm suddenly overwhelmed with pity. He looks so lonely sitting there sweating torrents, a veritable Niagara, even with a collar four times too big. With that turkey neck, he'd do better with a thirty-two. I'll bet people ignore him completely waiting in line—and he's probably the one who says excuse me.

I pick up my aperitif.

"Cheers."

His rear end rises off the sofa.

"To your health, Mademoiselle . . ."

"Puisset," I say, "Jacqueline Puisset."

I've decided to be the picture of friendliness.

"And to yours, Monsieur Bertovin."

Coughing.

"Bertouin."

"I'm sorry, to your health, Monsieur Bertouin."

Sebastian rolls on the floor in hysterics, looks at me, and yells:

"Did you hear Tata? She called him Bertovin!"

Explosion of mirth. The others chime in:

"Bertovin; Bertovin!"

François slaps at random at the bouncing rear ends.

"Go to your rooms, kids!"

Still out of control, the eldest looks at me.

"It's not Bertovin, it's Beethoven! Hey, you called Beethoven?"

I feel uncontrollable laughter rising up in me, submerging the pity. Noëlle beats the scoundrels back to their den.

I'd like to say something, but after all that, now I really don't know what his name is.

"Oh, those kids!"

He politely excuses them with a wave of his limp hand and adds:

"They're very lively."

"Yes," François says, "in that respect we can't complain."

Noëlle comes back, gracious, spontaneous, mundane. She drives me crazy with her lady-of-the-house act! As usual she is ravishing tonight. But enough of that, we have established once and for all that Noëlle is ravishing.

"Dinner is served."

Here I am next to . . . uh . . . it's something like
Beethoven, not far from Bertovin . . .

"My sister-in-law has a bookstore," François says.

What's-his-name looks up and exclaims as though
he'd just been told I was the principal dancer of the
Bolshoi:

"Oh, wonderful! Bravo!"

I must make an effort.

"Do you like to read?"

"Very much," he says, "very, very much."

I bet he's going to say it again.

"Very much."

I knew it. Now he's going to thoughtfully add that
unfortunately, he just doesn't have enough time.

"Unfortunately, I just don't have enough time to
enjoy this activity."

There it is. Way to go, Brenatus!

"Because it certainly is an activity, isn't it, Mademoiselle Puisset?"

Well I'll be, he remembered my name. Lucky
man!

"Yes indeed, it certainly is one."

The conversation is taking a passionate turn.
Let's give it a little punch:

"Indeed it is."

Silence.

They could say *something,* the two matchmakers.

"This rabbit is delicious," Mr. Nameless remarks.

"Oh, really," Noëlle whimpers, "I'm so glad you
like it, Monsieur Bertouin."

That's it, Bertouin. I've got it this time and I'm
holding on to it, Bertouin.

"And your work, do you enjoy it, Monsieur . . ."

It's incredible. I've never heard of such a short memory!

"Well, we have a good team, and then, there are certain responsibilities that . . ."

There goes old Chopin launching into a justification of the middle-class executive and the difficulties in setting up an insurance contract.

"Would you like some cheese?"

I get up.

"I'll help clear the table."

No doubt about it, What's-his-name is getting more boring by the minute. In the kitchen Noëlle is preparing the cheese, sour-faced:

"Not a real dazzler, huh?"

"What *is* his name?" I ask her. "I really can't remember!"

Noëlle picks up a stack of plates, puts it down, and ages fifteen years in a tenth of a second.

"I can't believe it," she yelps. "I knew it before you asked me."

"We could check his raincoat. I'm sure he's got his papers."

Noëlle jumps.

"Don't you dare do such a thing! You think he'll have a cup of coffee?"

"Probably not—maybe a very light Sanka."

Noëlle grabs her sister's arm and squeezes frantically with hope in her eyes.

"Vintoben! It's Vintoben!"

Jacqueline shakes her head sadly.

"Absolutely not. Hurry up, I'm sure François is asleep by now. Resistance is short with the nameless man."

The two sisters pile up the dirty plates. Jacqueline slides a Camembert onto the tray and smiles sadly.

"You did invite him because of me, didn't you?"

Embarrassed, Noëlle opens her arms wide, suddenly awkward.

"You know we mean well . . . but, well, from the description I knew it wouldn't work. I told François, but you never know. . . ."

She seems a little sorry, like every time. The worst part is that I'm the one who has to cheer her up.

"I don't think I'll marry this one. I'd never be able to remember my own name."

"Timhoven!" Noëlle shouts.

François's head pops in, furious.

"We having cheese or not? What are you doing in here, telling jokes?"

Noëlle rushes up and grabs her husband.

"What is your friend's name?"

"What friend?"

"The guest."

"At the office we call him the doormat, because he's a little obsequious. In fact, this may surprise you, but I can't remember his name."

Jacqueline feels content watching them laugh. She loves them both in spite of their mania for introductions. She loves them very, very much, as Bertini would say.

Who said, who would dare to say, I'm a lonely woman?

"I'm going to see the children . . . just for a minute."

There are evenings like that when life comes easy, when she's relaxed, at ease with herself. It's not even sure that tomorrow she'll have the same face.

"Tata, will you play car with us?"

Tonight Jacqueline Puisset is playing car.

"Sebastian, what was the man's name again?"

chapter seven

"Let him sit on your coat," Jacqueline says. "Otherwise he won't see a thing."

Noëlle sighs as her son gets up. She folds the heavy fabric and continues complaining—she hasn't stopped since they left the house.

"Oh, hush," Jacqueline says. "After all, it's his birthday."

"It certainly is. That's why we're here."

Jacqueline shrugs her shoulders. Next to her, her eldest nephew's feet dangle in the air. He is obviously delighted. He has been six for fifteen minutes.

"Does it start soon?"

"A few more minutes."

We've been talking about this for quite some time. Noëlle and François did their best to avoid it. They had plenty of alternate suggestions:

"What about a nice bicycle? Wouldn't you like that? With inflatable tires and everything?"

"No."

"Or some American jeans with top-stitching?"

"No."

"Lead soldiers? Cowboys and Indians?"

"No."

One evening, weakened by these stubborn refusals, in a moment of desperate generosity, François suggested:

"What about an electric train with detachable wagons?"

"No."

Thinking it over ten seconds, André added:

"For Christmas."

"We're not talking about Christmas, we're talking about your birthday."

"For my birthday, I want to go . . ."

François dropped his arms in capitulation.

"Okay, okay, if that's what you want, you can go."

Jacqueline looks behind her. It's an impressive place, just about full tonight; she's never been there before.

She leans over the kid's head, toward her sister:

"In any case, it was nice of you to think of me. It's just the kind of show that fills me with enthusiasm."

"Well, François can't stand it," Noëlle whispers, "and I didn't want to come alone."

Jacqueline crosses and recrosses her legs. The evening of her dreams: do the bills for the store, then a scotch, a salad, a bath, and a hundred pages in the book she's been trying to finish for two weeks. Oh well, it's for André. After all, he's her godson.

The lights dim.

"It's gonna start!" the boy explains.

Jacqueline perceives the greatest possible joy and anticipation in the tiny body vibrating in the seat next to her.

After all, if he likes it, that's great; anyway, it's not all that bad.

Under the spotlight a man in a white shirt smiles, and Jacqueline jumps: it's Monsieur Langaret, the one who buys the spy novels on sale.

A voice echoes through the loudspeakers, and applause explodes behind them.

"To start off with tonight, a great featherweight match between José Carnero and . . ."

Dumbfounded, Jacqueline Puisset watches the wrestlers bounce around a few inches away. Of course, François did his best—front row, if you please.

"Tata, is that Carnero?"

Jacqueline nods. Voices resonate from behind.

"Kill 'im, José!"

"You got 'im, no sweat!"

Gong.

Jacqueline jumps. José's adversary, furry as a chimpanzee, flings José Carnero over his hip onto the mat and takes him in a wristlock.

André bounces up and down three times.

"Get 'im José!"

Noëlle grabs him.

"Calm down."

José Carnero frees himself from a kidney grip and jumps like a baby goat from one corner to the other as the crowd goes wild.

"My God," Jacqueline shudders, "and there's six more to go."

chapter eight

PHILIPPE LIPINCHKY takes off his turtleneck with no great enthusiasm and folds his pants before hanging them up. At least another hour. His is the big match.

Dantron is already there.

"You going back to Paris tonight? I've got a friend who's gonna drive me up to Montpellier, if you wanna go."

Philippe hesitates. He'd save a day that way, but . . . well, no, his room is already paid for and he'd rather take his time.

"Thanks, but I think I'll sleep here."

Dantron grins.

"Who with?"

He's a good guy, Dantron, a good wrestler, about thirty pounds on the heavy side, but he's got style and talent. One slight flaw in the picture: women. He seduces them all; not one has resisted since Lover Dantron appeared on the face of the earth.

But then, with that Roman profile and triangular thorax, who could resist?

"In Saint-Brieuc I had three of 'em waiting in line. They had to flip a coin to see who'd go first."

Léon Cro-Magnon mumbles as he finishes his crossword puzzle:

"What about in Barcelonnette? Tell us what happened in Barcelonnette."

Philippe groans. Anything but that. Too late, Dantron's already into it.

"A duchess, not even thirty, with a body I've never seen the likes of."

"And you, of all people," Léon whispers as he fills in a six-letter word.

"Yeah, like you say, I've seen my share. Anyway, there she is waiting for me in a Lancia, a pearl-gray Lancia. I mean, she had class. She was driving. It was too much. She hardly had time to shift gears what with massaging my pectorals."

"And then?" Léon asks.

"So we get there, I pick her up, literally carry her into the room, open the door. I'm looking for the sack and what do I find?"

"A wrestling ring," Philippe says.

Dantron stops cold.

"I already told you?"

"What d'ya think?" Léon says.

"You guys disappoint me. You know what? You're real good guys and all that, but there's one thing you lack, and that's poetry."

Léon stands up, all 215 pounds of him, and caresses his bald head, like a polished marble block.

"You're right, man, we're brutes."

Philippe slips into his cherry-red leotard. "I'm

taking off for a two-week vacation in Tunisia Monday. Gonna do the 'Relax and Enjoy' Club. Anybody interested?"

Dantron rolls his eyes.

"You kiddin'? I did that in '71—never did sleep alone. There were girls coming in a dozen at a time."

"What about you, Léon?" Philippe says. "You ever done it?"

Léon folds his newspaper laconically.

"To each his own, my man, to each his own."

"And now, the match we have all been waiting for, a shattering Titan clash, World Champion in all categories, Lover Dantron, against the most hated, the most despicable man of all national and international rings, I mean Mephisto King!"

Lights. Whistles.

Jacqueline blinks, in a daze. André's body vibrates against her like a chord. Through the chaos of music and spotlights emerges a kind of overstuffed god, a Viking who's eaten too many milk products. He steps through the ropes. The audience roars, everybody's for him. He pivots, arms in the air, a friendly, handsome, seductive, dimpled hulk of muscle and cellulite.

"And now . . ."

The atrocious mask. André grabs Tata by the neck.

"He's a bastard, that one!"

Philippe goes by, ferocious.

Jacqueline shivers and winks at her sister, who pulls her crossed ankles in under the seat as the red cape from Hell sweeps by her.

Jacqueline gets a bird's-eye view of the dorsals

rolling under the skin. Impressive. The long painted dog teeth add a lot.

"You'll see," André says, "he's a real bastard."

"Don't talk like that and don't forget it's just a game."

"He's a bastard, I tell ya, I've seen him on TV, he's a real bastard."

Jacqueline admires her nephew. At his age, the sight of a monster like that would have given her a good six months of nightmares.

Mephisto King does three kneebends and shakes the ropes violently.

Not thrilled about Tunisia, but it's an opportunity. And I'll take my paints. Apparently at dusk the sun on the white villages is pretty impressive; it'll be inspiring. I'll bring back a few watercolors. It's too bad Maman doesn't want to go. I don't know how I'll ever capture the red sky on the white-washed walls . . . it must be even tougher than painting flowers. . . .

Gong.

"Bastard!"

That kid can really yell. He oughta be in bed this time of night.

Dantron starts him off in a double nelson. Lipinchky pulls out of it, gets taken in a scissors, shakes loose, and realizes that Loverboy is already puffing like an ox. Philippe acquiesces to Dantron's pinfall and finds himself flat on the mat to the delight of the fans in the pit.

If that's what makes them happy, why not? Get dragged around on the mat for two, three minutes; it'll give me a little rest.

Doesn't last long. Muscles flexed to the breaking

point, Philippe takes his man in a hold a bird could get out of. Dantron stoically endures nonexistent pain, his jaw locked.

André shakes his fist, tears in his eyes.

"Bastard!"

"He'll get out of it," Jacqueline says, "don't worry."

Dantron suffers heroically.

Merciless, Mephisto King kneads the fist of the doughy Viking.

"A half-hour match."

Completely dazed, Dantron wavers on his feet. For thirty minutes he's been victim to all the low blows, the nastiest imaginable treatment.

One last chop, he pirouettes off balance, and the ring trembles under the fall of the massive, quivering belly.

"One . . . two . . . three . . . four . . ."

The spy novel enthusiast counts.

Nine: Dantron is up, Mephisto attacks; he guards the blow, comes back with a forearm smash . . . splash . . . the badman's horizonal body glides through the air and lands.

André shoots for the ceiling like a Ping-Pong ball propelled by a fountain of water.

"Get 'im!"

Dantron's letting loose now. He lifts the 240 pounds of Satan's helper, tosses them into the air, catches them. He plays a little with the give in the ropes, then propels the masked man out of the ring. Philippe leaps wildly through the air, trying to gain control, but Dantron pushed too hard, or else he lifted himself too much—instead of landing just outside the ring, the wrestler is flying. The bookseller sees the mass of flesh enlarge above her and collapse with all its weight on the front row of seats, which in turn collapses. The crowd jumps up to see.

Fists and feet flying, André punches the sweaty body of the monster from Hell.

"Bastard!"

The people behind laugh.

Philippe gets up.

"Excuse me . . ."

He fell right on the lap of a very pale lady with closed eyes, who whispers:

"It's nothing."

Dantron is triumphant up above. The referee is counting. Should go back up, give 'em five more minutes of spectacle, but this lady is really pale.

Noëlle is rubbing her elbow.

"You okay, Jacqueline?"

Jacqueline looks again at the horror mask leaning toward her.

"Did I hurt you?"

The voice is surprising. It's true, there must be a person under there.

She tries to wiggle the toes of her right foot without success. It doesn't hurt. I haven't felt anything since the shock.

Jacqueline Puisset looks at Philippe Lipinchky and, as though asking him to please pass the salt, calmly remarks:

"My leg is broken."

The colossus kneels down.

"Shit," he murmurs in a thoughtful tone.

Philippe Lipinchky and Jacqueline Puisset have just exchanged their first words.

André summons the strength of his sixty pounds and lets loose a left uppercut to Mephisto King's liver.

"Bastard!" he bellows. "That's Tata! You fell on Tata!"

"Don't move," Philippe says. "The doc'll be here in a second. Could you hold the kid back though?"

Noëlle holds her son against her; Jacqueline quietly faints; Lipinchky, counted out, scratches his head. Dantron parades in triumph. The crowd is up and cheering: Good has won out again tonight.

Outside, a warm summer rain has begun to fall, the kind that makes the mornings fresh and clear, that empties even the deepest recesses of the sky, a cleansing rain, efficient and resonant, dropping its wet chords on the dry pavement, streaming across the posters where a huge-muscled devil in a red cape seems to defy the universe with his bulging biceps.

chapter nine

THERE is the distinct odor of fresh plaster of paris in the room. Solving this mystery is as easy as lifting the blanket. A fractured tibia, a clean break, no cracks—a delight for the radiologist.

"Did an anvil drop on your leg? It's rare to see a hematoma like that."

"It wasn't an anvil, it was Mephisto King."

He whistled, obviously without a clue as to what a Mephisto King was, except that it must be something heavy.

So, two days in the hospital to recuperate, which I don't really need, then Tuesday I get out. Six weeks of hobbling around the store in a cast. Fabienne'll have to pick me up in her car.

Noëlle should be here soon. What an evening! The ambulance just for me, headlights tearing through the night, rain on the stretcher, just like in the movies. Everything but the motorcycle hoods and gangsters. But there *were* wrestlers, my frantic

sister, and André. He'll remember this birthday all
right. It'll be an easy reference point in the family
from now on— "You know, it was before his sixth
birthday, before Tata was squashed by the big guy
with the mask."

It's not really so bad here.

I don't know why I say that; it's not so great
either. Well, it's a hospital room, no more, no less:
a bed, two chairs, a sink, and hospital green everywhere. It's weird having this weight at the end of my
leg. What dreams I've had of waking up in rooms
like this. The sun barely up, the air smelling of
flowers and ether—even to the point of imagining
the odors, the colors of the walls. My head wrapped
in bandages, like Ramses II or the Invisible Man.
Everything is still, when suddenly I sense a presence
and hands touching me lightly.

"Who are you?"

A compassionate, professional male voice:

"Don't move, keep eyes closed."

The hands unwrap the bandages, the mummy is
unwound. Attentive, expert nurses stand by.

My eyes are free, I start to shake.

"Open."

I look at him; he is handsome. He looks like my
neighbor, but twenty years older. He's quite splendid, my neighbor—another unrequited love.

He's smiling, tan in his white jacket. I already
feel something starting between us.

"Look at yourself."

A mirror appears, reflecting the wall, the angle
of the bed, the pillow, and stopping at my eyes: I
am beautiful. The rest varies according to my
moods. Either he kisses me tenderly or rudely chases

away the nurses, bringing his lips passionately to mine.

Here I am, finally, in this room I've dreamt of a thousand times . . . for a broken leg! Life is ridiculous.

I wonder what I would have looked like with parallel eyes—nothing to write home about, but still . . .

Deep down, I've never gotten over it. But people who talk about getting over things are never walleyed.

In fifteen minutes Noëlle will be here.

It's the first time it's happened to me, but also, officially, there was not enough room between the spectators and the ring.

I heard it crack. Sounded weird, like a stubborn door . . . *clack!*

There's not much I can do. My insurance will pay.

Of course I could go by the hospital, since my train isn't till four o'clock. I didn't see her too well, but she seemed nice. A little something with her eye, of course . . . but what's nice is that she didn't insult me. Just the necessary: "My leg is broken."

A strict minimum. Anyway, she didn't seem to hold it against me, which is rare, not like the little kid who was calling her Tata. Right in the ribs. He hurt me more than Dantron did during the whole match!

What do I do?

I could take her some geraniums, but I'd look ridiculous holding a pot of geraniums. And she undoubtedly doesn't like them. Geraniums are great to paint in watercolors, but you have to admit they're nothing special in real life. Even the smell is bad, sort of suffocating—the leaves smell like dried dirt. In a closed room it must be stifling. I've already broken her leg, it's better if I don't asphyxiate her!

Just bad luck to land on her—a woman's more breakable. Anyway, you can't exactly choose. . . .

This whole thing made me sleep badly. That noise kept running through my head. Have to think about something else. I'm gonna shave and think about Tunisia.

Damn it! What am I gonna do in Tunisia all alone? Maman was great last Sunday: "You'll be able to meet some new people." Yeah, I know what she's talking about. She acts like I'm eighteen years old and a hundred ten pounds.

Hey, speaking of new people, I met one last night, in a direct style all my own: crack! She'll remember me all right, my new acquaintance. I won't have passed by unnoticed.

Tunisia . . .

If I hadn't already gotten the tickets, I'd stay home. What the hell am I gonna do with all those suntanned guys around?

I think I'll just take a walk around the town— three hours to kill, I'll take it slow, get some fresh air. I'm not gonna go close myself up in some hospital room with some lady who's gonna let me have it.

Avoid complications, Toto, avoid complications. It's healthier.

chapter ten

Room 53.

Philippe Lipinchky knocks and listens, looking terribly embarrassed.

"Come in, it's open."

Shit, she's expecting someone.

He pushes the door open. Jacqueline's eyes widen.

A mastodon.

Philippe attempts a smile. God, she really is wall-eyed.

"I'm the one who . . . last night . . ."

"Yes, I . . . uh . . . that is, I recognized you."

Jacqueline's hands outline an enormous shape in the air.

I wonder if he wasn't better with the mask on. A nice voice—that struck me, not as much as the rest, of course, but . . .

The wrestler shifts his feet and holds out a package.

"I know it doesn't help much, but, well, I wanted to say I'm sorry, so I brought you this. Since I didn't know what you like, I chose the winner of the prix Goncourt."

"Excellent choice. You couldn't have done better."

Philippe feels reassured seeing her laugh. She must like to read. For once he's hit the target.

"Sit down, it's nice of you to come. You have a minute, don't you?"

He placed one-fourth of his rear end on the vinyl armchair, knees squeezed tight.

"It's ridiculous. In a twenty-year career it's never happened to me. I know that won't put your tibia back together, but . . ."

"Ah, then you know it's the tibia?"

"Yeah, I asked a guy in white in the hall."

That's nice. God, those shoulders! It's unusual, a man built like that. He wouldn't be bad if his face weren't so squashed—looks like a baked potato.

"That was my first wrestling match. We went for my little nephew's birthday."

Philippe's hand goes up.

"That boy could have a career in the ring! I've still got bruises."

They laugh and look at each other. Quite a picture—something of a horror show. One eye in one direction, a plastered leg in the other, three hundred fifty pounds, and a baked potato. We could play a great comic *Romeo and Juliet*.

Philippe gets up.

"Don't cry," he says. "Six weeks and you'll be dancing. The guy told me."

Now I start laughing. My word, I'm going crazy.

"I'm laughing because when I cry, I'm even less attractive. It's hard to believe, but it's true!"

She searches frantically for a handkerchief.

"You're not unattractive," Philippe says. "I . . ."

I can't really tell her she's beautiful; she's not stupid enough to believe that.

"Look at me, I've got a face like a boiled potato."

"Baked," Jacqueline says.

Philippe freezes, lets out a sigh that could knock down a wall, and slaps his forehead with the palm of his hand.

"My God, that changes everything!"

She laughs and looks at him.

Having a sense of humor isn't limited to scrawny men.

"What do you do for a living?"

I can't believe it—this sounds like a pickup.

"I have a bookstore."

Plaf! Right on target, as I was saying.

He takes the book from the table and gets up.

"I'll be right back with chocolates."

Something strange happens now, a kind of reflex: He puts his hand on the book and I put my hand on his.

"No, I assure you, I'm happy to have it."

He shrugs his shoulders.

"You must have a store full of the prix Goncourt."

"About one hundred fifty."

This is a man's hand under my palm. It's finally happened, my dear.

He sits back down.

"I was going to bring you flowers, but then you would have been a florist."

"And you? Why wrestling?"

I feel good—it's not really so tough to chat with women. Maman would be happy if she saw me.

"Well, I guess I was cut out for it pretty young. What with everyone telling me I had the wrestler's build. I learned some of the tricks, made some friends. I liked the atmosphere and eventually turned pro, but . . ."

"But what?"

Strange, this woman. When she asks questions, there's something encouraging about it—a painless birth: push and you'll have a beautiful baby.

"What I would have liked is to paint. I do a little bit at home."

"What do you paint?"

Ah, my geraniums. How to explain my geraniums, the nuances. . . . I'll never have time and I haven't even asked her if it hurts.

"I meant to ask, is it painful?"

"Deathly."

He smiles. It's funny to see hands that you've touched. It makes them look different, more tender, more. . . . Take it easy, Jacqueline, what's going on here? No alliances. Your life is set out and so is his.

"What troubles me most is my vacation. I was supposed to leave in a week and . . ."

"Where are you going?"

"To my sister's, in the mountains, not too far. We were going to redo the ceilings, but I think I'll have to restrict myself to knitting."

"Me, I'm going to Tunisia," he mumbles.

Lugubrious.

"You don't seem too thrilled."

"No, the more I think about it, the less I want to go."

She's really laughing. I've never made a woman laugh so much. Of course, it's also the first time I've demolished a woman's tibia. She gets all the firsts.

What if I took her to Tunisia, this bookseller? I could carry her to the beach and. . . . Go ahead, do it, Phi-Phi, just one sentence, do it, ask her. I'm dripping wet. Do it, you jerk.

"Would you . . ."

Knock, knock. A bright-eyed brunette storms in, arms flung in the air.

"My God, Jacqueline, when I think of it! But everything's okay, they told me. Here, let me kiss you. You don't have a fever, do you? When do you get out? André's in the hall. He wanted to come in, but it's not allowed. Can you believe such a thing? François is just frantic. We didn't sleep a wink—that huge monster falling right on you!"

Jacqueline points her finger.

"I'd like you to meet . . ."

"Philippe," says Philippe. "Philippe Lipinchky."

The bright eyes adjust, then widen. Obviously she can't imagine what this blushing mountain could possibly be doing in the hospital room of Jacqueline Puisset, the manless woman.

"Noëlle Louberan, my sister."

Philippe offers his hand; the sister is shaking it, completely perturbed, when a voice explodes:

"It's Mephisto!"

Through the opening in the door comes André's accusing finger. Philippe recoils strategically, causing the two women to laugh.

Noëlle clasps her hands like Bernadette Soubi-
rous.

"My God, it's you! I didn't recognize you without
the mask."

"That's comforting," Philippe says.

"He brought me the prix Goncourt," Jacqueline
says.

The kid visually squeezes the muscles bulging
under the suit.

"Did you do it on purpose last night?"

Cry of horror from Noëlle.

"Now you just hush! Kiss Tata and go play in
the hall or else you'll have a broken leg yourself."

Suspicious, the boy keeps his eyes glued on Philippe.

"You did it on purpose, I saw it."

"It's true," Philippe admits. "I do that almost
every match, but usually I don't land on the spectators."

"I knew it," murmurs the kid.

"That's nice," Noëlle says. "Here's François."

The door opens. François Louberan walks
straight into Mephisto's chest, looks up, and walks
out.

"Excuse me."

"It's here," Noëlle shouts. "Here, let me introduce you. Monsieur Lipinchky-who-broke-Jacque-
line's-leg, my husband, François."

In a daze François grasps the hand in front of
him.

"Oh! You're the one who . . ."

"I heard a knock," Jacqueline says. "Come in."

In comes a quivering young girl. Twenty years

old, shapely legs, brilliant lips, wavy hair, bulging T-shirt, tight jeans; it's Fabienne.

Jacqueline panics.

"Did you close the store?"

"No, no, Madame Rancier's taking my place. I wanted to know what I should order, because the salesmen from Julliard and Grasset are waiting and. . ."

François is talking to his wife; André's giving Philippe a hard time, backing him farther and farther into the corner.

Why don't I go now? I've got to go now. I've got nothing else to do here. . . .

"Could you have won if you'd wanted to last night?"

The door opens. Philippe is stupefied. It's incredible how much this guy looks like Trotsky, even with an armful of mimosas.

"I came as soon as I found out about it. They told me at the bookstore."

"That's really nice of you, Monsieur Trotsky."

Jacqueline gasps under the yellow flowers.

"Oh, I'm sorry, it just slipped out. I hope I . . ."

Trotsky smiles at her gently.

"Not at all, it's very nice. Of course I know about it. Somehow it makes us more . . . intimate."

The chief of the Soviets lifts his wire-rimmed glasses toward Philippe in an expression combining sincere admiration and total confusion.

"Monsieur Trotsky, I'd like you to meet . . ."

"It's Mephisto," André says. "He breaks legs, he can break anything, huh, can't you break anything you want?"

"Ah, ah!" Trotsky says.

He coughs, nods all around, seems atrociously embarrassed for a moment, then lets out:

"I wanted to read you a few sonnets from this little collection, but I see you have a lot of visitors, so it'll be for next time."

"No," Jacqueline says, "please do, I'm sure everyone would enjoy it."

Trotsky blushes, the wrestler seems somewhat suffocated, François sits down, Noëlle shuts up, Fabienne drops her jaw as usual, hypnotized.

"It's an elegy from Ghylaine de Valmondois, 1846 to 1904. Here it is."

I could be in an iron lung with nozzles in every limb, and he'd come read to me.

> Soft breezes of distracted languor,
> The specter of your eyes fills the mist,
> Oh savage beauty, forgotten by the tomb. . . .

Incorrigible Trotsky. . . . I don't know much about him really. Except that he's about as much of a loner as you can be, and that he reads his poems only to me, his bookseller.

Philippe makes me want to laugh—he hasn't taken his eyes off of him.

> And caresses the cheek of the conqueror
> with her palm.

He shuts the book; that way we know it's over.

"Marvelous!" exclaims Fabienne.

The others shift their feet, utter half sentences, a few grunts and sighs. Jacqueline sinks into her pillows.

Philippe, being the closest, takes the mimosas from her. Two nurses come in and clear a path.

"You have quite a crowd here, Mademoiselle Puisset."

"Glory at last," Jacqueline murmurs.

Fatigue has hit, tangibly. Noëlle is holding André in her arms.

Philippe leans over.

"I'm going to leave you now. I've got to go. . . ."

I will not feel abandoned because a gorilla is returning to his native forest. It's too stupid, too . . . I don't know what. It's ridiculous, all these people around me . . .

"Do you live far away?"

"Paris, but . . . I'll write to find out how you are."

He'll never do it. A hundred to one.

"I wanted to tell you again . . ."

"No, please don't say you're sorry again. Send me some postcards from Tunisia."

Go ahead, say it. With all those people, the sister, the nephew, the brother-in-law, the customer, the salesgirl, the nurses all standing there, ears perked, tell her any way, tell her you'll take her.

"I hope you get well soon."

"Thank you for the book."

He shakes hands in a dream . . . the kid's minuscule hand.

Here's the hall. . . . What else could I do? I couldn't stand there all day with the whole family at the bedside. Tomorrow it's back to Paris for a match at Nanterre. Anyway, take it easy, she's not exactly the girl of your dreams. Friendly, nice, courageous, you name it, but you can't exactly call that eye fetching—that would be pushing it a bit.

Outside, the palm trees are enormous against the blue sky. Last night they said on the radio it was cold in Paris, foggy too. . . .

On to the train. So long, beautiful country I hardly even saw—not even enough to leave a memory.

chapter eleven

HOSPITAL nights have a bluish cast.

The last TVs have just been turned off. They stayed pretty late, Noëlle the last to go. She arranged it to get the last word in.

"It was nice of him to come, huh? What did you think of him?"

"Not great to look at."

She didn't go so far as to say "Beauty isn't everything," but it was close.

"Well, but you're picky."

No doubt the half-dozen horrible creatures she tried to hook me up with sprung to mind, but I was tired, I wanted to be alone, and I must have been more brutal than I meant to be.

"I'm not picky, I just feel fine the way I am."

"Yeah, yeah," she said—just the thing to drive me crazy. It's the tone of voice.

"Don't give me your 'yeah, yeahs.' I tell you I'm just fine the way I am."

"It's not true."

Never gives up, Mother Noëlle. I used to call her that just to see her go wild with rage.

"It is true."

She blushed, put on her social worker's look, and decreed:

"Perhaps it's true, but it's not healthy."

I'd have sat down if I hadn't already been lying down.

"What isn't healthy?"

She turns scarlet. I know exactly what she means, but I want to hear her say it.

"Being alone, it isn't healthy."

In these situations my machiavellian instincts emerge. With the voice of an angel I ask:

"Why isn't it healthy?"

Deeper scarlet.

"Sexually."

"What do you mean, sexually?"

She explodes.

"You know perfectly well what I mean. For a woman to blossom, she must . . ."

"Must what?"

"Shit."

"It's been a while since I've gotten the blossoming woman bit. Are you a blossomed woman?"

She jumps up, ready to give me her joy-in-life routine, but I cut her off.

"Listen, if you feel up to trying your luck with Mephisto, I could send him your address."

She laughs and kisses me.

"Might not be a bad idea. Those big guys are usually tender-hearted; it'd be a change of air for me."

"You might blossom."

"See you tomorrow, old girl. I'll go by the book-store in the afternoon."

It was just a joke. I don't even have his address. It's true, though, it's not healthy. That is, it's not unhealthy, but it's true that sometimes. . . . Oh, for-get it.

I can see it now. Arriving with him in the morn-ing to open the store. "My God, did you see Made-moiselle Puisset? With a giant, no less. That's why she never married, couldn't find one big enough. It's perverse if you ask me. You never noticed she looks a little vicious there behind the cash register? Be-ware of snakes in tall grass."

Not all the old ladies in the windows are particu-larly nice. On park benches, or in the back rooms of corner groceries, they chitchat at a lively clip be-tween the green peppers and the eggplants. At night, when the heat has passed, they bring out their wicker chairs, and the tongues start wagging. They know everything; nothing gets by them. We live in such a closed community.

And then Sunday, after Mass—I see them from my window. I'm there too, looking out like an old gossip. There's the sky and the red tiles, and below in the winding streets, the incessant chatter of my fellow citizens. Small-town mania . . . I see them in groups; the men tip their hats, the kids pull up their socks. The ladies prance out of the luxury catering shops with their flat boxes stuffed with petits fours and Saint-Honoré pastries. The salesgirl makes huge bows of violet ribbon like hydrangeas. What are they going to say, all those people? There's never been such a scandal in this town. Sure, the mechanic's daughter had some adventures with one of the lower officials at City Hall, but a bookseller's different. She's expected to be serious her entire life, otherwise people will buy their best-sellers somewhere else. . . .

Sometimes I can't stand this town that I love. In boarding school I hated those avenues where we spent empty Sundays walking in rows: the Cours Lazare, the avenue des Pyrénées . . . long beaches of boredom bordered by disdainful houses.

I can hear them now, those ladies from the fashionable neighborhood—a lovely concert between the old fort and the Dagobert Barracks.

André's the only one who'd be thrilled. A wrestler uncle—that's impressive for his pals.

Oh, hush, enough of this. A little discipline. You're forty years old, my dear.

I've got to go to sleep. So much has happened since last night. I'm sure there are lots of women who like the traveling type.

It's terrible, Tunisia. I didn't want to be discouraging, but it'll be horrible—flat beaches, couscous three times a day, more Parisians per square mile than on the Grands Boulevards. . . . Fabienne told me all about it. Of course, she loved it. She must have had fifty tan young men chasing after her—volleyball and tango. Not exactly for the tibia-breakers. . . . I said, forget it!

In fact, this cast is quite convenient. It'll be a real vacation, plenty of pampering. I'll settle in on the terrace with my book, my knitting . . . knitting . . . book . . . tea at five o'clock. Who said I'm not a blossomed woman?

Almost one in the morning and I can't sleep.

Over four thousand books on reserve and I'm re-
duced to reading the prix Goncourt. Oh well.

Jacqueline Puisset turns on the light, puffs up her
pillow, lifts herself up with a few contortions, dragging five pounds of plastered leg, and opens her
book with a sigh. Three lines and her mind wanders.
She sits immobile, staring into the blue-tinted night,
the color of the softened lights in the corridors of
the trains rolling this minute toward Paris.

chapter twelve

ROBERT-ODILON TROUSSELIER is a man with two peculiarities: one, to be the only person alive to spend six months of every year at the shore of one of the warmest seas on the globe, in constant sunshine, and stay perpetually porcelain white, like a sink; two, to be a most versatile instructor, specialized in the artistic disciplines. He covers them all, excelling in each one more than the last. He teaches everything from lithography, serigraphy, all the graphic arts, to flute, weaving, classical and modern guitar, kite making, photography, and folk dance—specializing in the bourrée Auvergnate. From April to September he flutters from one workshop to another, dynamically animating generations of vacationers, whom he exhausts in a matter of weeks. But most remarkable is his weakness for a certain occupation that demands by far his most serious attention: pottery.

For Trousselier, human nature is divided into two categories: potters and nonpotters. When he runs out of students, Robert-Odilon charges in amongst the fake Arabic earthenware of the dining hall, scans out some loner twiddling his thumbs or reading, and drags him into the studio. He recites his poetic formulas of the antique and secular gestures of those who work with and give life to the earth, and from whom we owe it to ourselves to rediscover this eternal art.

Within a half hour the victim has two options: attempt to swim back to Europe or find himself slithering in glaze in front of an enormous, pivoting, droplet-spewing mudpile.

At that moment Trousselier takes out the minuscule notebook that has made thousands of tourists tremble and articulates the dreaded, always identical sentence:

"I see you seem to like it. I'll sign you up for the rest of your stay. We start every morning at nine."

This particular morning, as a white sun rises in a sky as blue as the sea and a limitless boredom coats the vacation camp of Boukhari, Trousselier makes his way to his beloved studio. Its architecture evokes at once a fortified mosque and a roadside supermarket.

Mme. Formoisan is already there.

Mme. Formoisan is a faithful student. Every morning she's there, behind her wheel. She's been coming to Boukhari for three years and she's never missed a session in the studio. She is hoping, in the years to come, to be able to fabricate a pot for her cacti—quite an audacious enterprise, for despite three years' effort a curious phenomenon always occurs: Mme. Formoisan leans to the left. All her vases, cups, and cylinders invariably lean to the left. Trousselier has checked the footings, given special lessons, explained, demonstrated . . . useless, everything leans. The worst is when she tries to correct it, because then the finished product takes the shape of a lopsided cone, amazingly limp and morose.

Having greeted the elderly lady and once more suggested raising the right support, Odilon decides to recruit more students.

A new shipment arrived the day before yesterday. Damned if there won't be a pottery amateur among them.

Odilon avoids the already sizzling beach—it's murderous for his delicate epiderm. Anyway, he knows the beach is the chosen land of the nonpotters. It's the land of volleyballers, sand dune flirters, kids playing in the waves. The streets of the camp are more propitious to his hunt.

Odilon zigzags among the blockhouse-style bungalows, but the white streets are already empty. Desperately trying to resemble an Arabic village, the camp resembles only itself; that is, nothing.

The bar. Why not try the bar?

Odilon enters, blinking in the sudden obscurity, and zeroes in on his prey. He uses psychology, as he likes to put it. He can single out a bored man at a hundred yards.

There's no doubt that this man is bored beyond belief.

Undeniable proof: he's reading, and he's reading the prix Goncourt. Ten seconds of observation to perceive the dormant potter about to be initiated.

"Excuse me . . ."

Philippe looks up. A real bore, no doubt, but after all, it'll pass the time.

"Have a seat."

Odilon sits down and launches his attack with the profound conviction that Philippe will be putty in his hands within three minutes.

"I see you're all alone. I know, I know, the first contacts aren't so easy in a community like ours, but it's up to each of us to find the activity that suits him, and I'm here to counsel, to help you make this choice. In fact, it's actually quite simple. I'm sure, I'm certain even, that you would like to rediscover the antique and secular gestures of those who work with and give life to the glaze and . . ."

Philippe studies him and jumps up. My God, it's him! It's the potter!

Last evening flashes through the colossus's mind. At dinner, an old man in khaki shorts had approached his table with a hunted-down look. Philippe thought for a moment that he was going to say he'd just put a time bomb under the table. The old man had glanced behind him.

"You're new here?"

"Yes."

"Be careful. There's a really pale guy—don't let him get you. I got caught: six days of pottery—pure hell!"

His fingers were still going through the motions of manipulating some wretched substance while his mouth had twisted in total disgust.

"I got away, but I know he's looking for me. Excuse me."

Stooped over, the old man had taken two steps, turned back toward Philippe, and whispered into his ear:

"Warn the others."

Bless that old guy, he was right.

Odilon has already placed his white hand on the cover of his notebook.

"I'll sign you up now, to save time. We start at . . ."

Philippe looks at his watch.

"Oh no, it's stopped! What time is it?"

"Nine thirty-five," Odilon says. "I . . ."

"My bath," Philippe says. "Excuse me, it's a ritual."

He strides out, turns to the right, again to the right, right again, and cautiously pokes his head into the bar he just left. Odilon is gone.

Philippe sits down with a sigh.

Overwhelmingly bored. In that respect Odilon was on the mark. . . . And then, the first time he went into his room, he thought it was the bathroom, with the bed in the place of the bathtub. Fortunately it folds up; otherwise he'd have to brush his teeth sitting down. But the worst is the neighbors.

A young man to the left, always humming *Juanita Banana,* even in his sleep, which wouldn't be so bad if it weren't for the couple to the right. Those two are incredible—a fury of sexuality—opera singers making love as though interpreting *La Traviata* or *Rigoletto.* I've never felt so lonely as the last two night with those outbursts of libido. Makes no difference what time it is—they even set the alarm. Impossible to go back to sleep, for them and for me.

Three weeks of this diet and I'll lose fifty pounds.
I'll be ready for the featherweights.

My God, I didn't even see him! This guy's a
camouflage expert, literally blends into the wall.

The elderly antipottery man spots Philippe and
slaloms between tables, bent over like an old Indian.

"Did you see him?"

"He just left," Philippe says. "You can relax."

Raucous laughter followed by a fit of coughing.

"He's not the only one. Just because you've
avoided one doesn't mean you're safe. Have you
eaten in the main dining hall yet?"

"No, I . . ."

The old man raises his hands to his temples.

"You'll see! They literally attack. Last week some
guy wanted me to try water-skiing. With my throm-
bosis! And at forty-five francs an hour! He didn't
even ask me if I knew how to swim! And then the
waiters! Don't bother putting on a clean shirt for
dinner—you've got gravy stains before you can say
ouf! As for the folding beds, oolalalalalala! Have
you tried to unfold one?"

"Just one question: why do you come back every
year?"

The old man bursts out laughing, coughs, knocks
his knees, half-chokes to death, orders a lemonade,
scratches his head, glances cautiously about, on the
lookout as though someone were behind him, and
says:

"My daughter-in-law."

"I don't get it," Philippe says.

"She pays. It's her treat, as she puts it. You heard
me right: treat. The first time, when she paid for it,

I couldn't tell her I didn't like it. 'It's beautiful, Tunisia, eh, Gramps?' Oh, yes, it's beautiful. 'Well, then, I promise you'll go back next year.' Four years she's kept her word, the bitch. Four years of camp."

He wets his lips with lemonade and surreptitiously gestures with his fist at the retreating waiter.

"It's warm. They do it on purpose."

"Ask for some ice."

"So they can charge extra? No way."

Philippe glances at his watch. Two more hours before lunch, before the atrocious lunch, as the irascible old guy would say.

"I'm gonna take a walk. See you later on."

The old codger almost chokes on his lemonade.

"Oh, no doubt about that, there's no escape— that I can guarantee you. I've tried everything."

The shadow retreats to a blue border along the low walls, and the dry palm trees scrape the hot stones. I'll never make it. I'm not even up to getting out my paints. Haven't even completely unpacked— gives me less of the impression that I'm here. Maybe a little dip in the sea; after all, that's part of why I'm here.

I'm anxious to write this postcard, but I won't mail it for a few days, so as not to seem too much in a hurry. Have to think up something clever, not a "Bright sun, blue sea, having fun." No, something humorous, in good taste, and with a touch of sweetness . . . avoiding anything along the lines of "Better than having a broken leg." Have to be careful with the picture too: the two palm trees with the camel in the middle—that's for the guy who wants people to be absolutely sure he's not spending his vacation in the Loir-et-Cher. For Léon Cro-Magnon, I know just what he'd like . . . an Arabic woman . . . yeah, a moukère.

Philippe stops, breathless. A couple, between the dunes. The voices give them away. No question, this lady should try for the Opéra. Cheeks on fire, Philippe whistles nonchalantly as he passes the white rear end of his nextdoor neighbor.

How idiotic can you get: They are completely naked, making love right out in the open, get taken by surprise, and I'm the one who's embarrassed. It's incredible. Doesn't bother them a bit. If I were that guy, it'd take me a year to get over it. A question of generations.

Finally on the beach, flooded with mingling bodies, trembling in the vapors of suntan oil. Girls the color of fine gold gleam in pearls of water.

They're all there, roasting like partridges. Of course, I forgot to buy any cream. Maman even reminded me. If I stay it'll be sunstroke, not to mention a lobster burn. Then the skin will peel off in patches, which would really be a pity. Might make me ugly . . . very funny.

Not a square inch of shade. Might as well head back to the bar.

Philippe returns to the false village along the pseudo-streets. The cries of the volleyballers fade in the distance.

Noon, the hour when the sun strikes pure like a lead wire, no traces. A talented assassin.

chapter thirteen

"Look, man, the Dum-Dums may be a little too flashy, but with Chapman on drums, they get into some real 'feeling,' man. You heard 'I'm the King, O.K., Mummy?' It's their latest single."

"You're crazy, man, those guys are lightweights, really second rate, just like the Stones."

"The Stones second rate?"

"Yeah, man, they're lightweights compared to . . ."

"And you, with your hard rock and Roxy Music, you got somethin' heavier?"

"Excuse me, could you please pass the salt?"

"Sure, there's some heavy stuff there, but for a supple, instrumental kind of blues atmosphere with a sonorous context culminating without distortion, you gotta . . ."

"Don't make me laugh. What you're talking about is an electric Chicago style tonality with heavy metal rhythmic structures like with Billy Gibbons."

"Gibbons is trash, man, he copied everything he does from Brad Delp when he was with Lonesome Road."

"Could you please pass me the salt?"

"Lonesome Road's a bullshit band. You heard Mick Taylor? Now there's some good sixties rock. The riffs that guy comes up with, man . . ."

"What kinda ax you got?"

"A Black Sun, with fuzz tone, echo chamber, and . . ."

"I'd like the salt . . ."

"You gotta be kiddin'. He's small time, man. Anyway, Monkey Looley doesn't have a Black Sun; he's on drums and . . ."

Philippe swallows his cheese and gets up, his mouth full. Two more seconds and there would have been three casualties.

Martians. They didn't even see me. Two hundred forty pounds, over six foot five, and they didn't even see me. I could do a belly dance on the table and they wouldn't even notice.

Tonight I change tables. One night of Chicago-style folk chords and Mick Jagger in the echo chamber is enough. What the hell am I going to do this afternoon? It's too hot for a nap, and it's not going to take me three hours to write a postcard. . . . To think my pals envy me taking it easy in the sun!

A faint scraping sound to the left: the old man flees between the dried-out trunks of the palm trees. The vacationers leave in orderly groups to take up their afternoon activities. Philippe assumes a preoccupied air and slips away to the somewhat cooler shade of his bungalow. Melancholy waiters gather dishes from the deserted tables roasting in the sun.

The emptiness is deadly in the buzzing of the summer flies. Eleven days to go.

La Garenne. I'm the same height as my mother. I don't like the gardens in this neighborhood or the long dark streets giving off from the railroad tracks. When the Paris trains pass, the dishes vibrate in the old stone sinks.

One of Maman's friends lives here. We don't come very often.

I go up, knowing what's gonna happen. They're in there waiting for me, in the bushes. This time I refuse to hear them—there's gotta be some big noise that'll drown them out. Something's gotta happen this time. The door opens; the woman is there, smiling.

"Come say hello, girls."

I'm not gonna look at them, not this time. Oh God, I wish I didn't exist. Pity me, girls, pardon me for what I am, pardon my ugliness, but please, please . . .

They look at him burst out laughing.

Victoria blushes, suddenly helpless. I can't hear anything.

I never want to hear anything again.

I am not in the garden, I'm not anywhere. I never existed.

It's the little one who's gonna say it, I can tell from her eye, that enormous eye; nothing can make it blink. It'll pursue me to my death.

"Potato face," she says. "You look like a potato."

I run through the empty streets bordered by iron gates and sculptured hedges. I'm hardly twelve years old and . . .

Philippe sits up suddenly on his bed, streaming with sweat.

I've been having that dream for so long. It comes back all the time, like a refrain. Two little girls in a sad garden. It's so vivid. I knew they would, they said it, they say it, and they'll go on saying it till the end of time.

Beyond the mosquito net lies the moon-white village.

I'll never get to sleep now.

chapter fourteen

"TATA, it's the mailman."

Jacqueline wrinkles her brow.

"Don't talk to me, I'm counting my stitches."

The rope soles of his espadrilles unravel as he runs up the stones. Jacqueline blocks the stitch with her thumbnail on the steel needle and watches the boy climb the path. The hills are mauve, the countryside red, and a golden sun rains down on the round tiles. François has been sawing boards since dawn, his mouth full of nails; Noëlle is preparing a vegetable casserole as deep as a tomb. Tonight the Montpellier cousins arrive. Cousin Zelle will have in tow her usual collection of self-consciously nonchalant admirers whose days are spent in languishing postures in the shadow of the cool walls. Strange, that girl's passion for slow mammals requiring a supreme effort for minimal speech, and a pointless effort at that.

"Here, Tata."

The morning ritual. She sorts the mail: everything for Noëlle and François, everything for her . . . catalogues, bills, ciné-club programs. A filtered echo of life before vacation, and after . . .

A card from Nice. Jacqueline turns and yells:
"Noëlle, Renée is on the Côte d'Azur."

Noëlle's distant voice comes perfumed with fennel and laurel:
"She's always been an idiot."

Jacqueline laughs and scratches her knee above the cast. More bills. A letter from Fabienne. Lucky Fabienne, splendid Fabienne. She must have a lot more energy with me gone: doesn't have to go to the back room to redo her mascara and lipstick.

What does the Fatal Beauty have to say?

> I hope you're resting up and that the bone is healing. Here, we're selling a lot of guidebooks, as there are lots of people coming through. Yesterday there were even some Japanese people—and Perpignan is awfully far for them too.

She has a good sense of distance, that girl. She must have made quite a hit with the Japanese. I'm surprised she hasn't been whisked off to Tokyo yet by one of those guys loaded with cameras. If I'd had her physique I'd be on my fifteenth trip around the world with my twenty-fifth lover. She's so namby-pamby.

> Most of our regular customers have gone on vacation. I saw M. Javier who recites so well, but when he saw you weren't here, he left. And

I even had his order—*Shaded Paths* by Noémie de Chassereine. I ran after him, but he'd disappeared.

Dear old Trotsky. It's true he must miss me. It's hard to have no one to share your passions.

So I hope you're having good weather, and don't worry about the store, I'm here. Please get well quickly. A big hug.

Yours,
Fabienne

I like you a lot, Fabienne, and that's not easy since I would have liked so much to be you. . . . What's this? A sunset on the sea? Yes. In fact, it's marked underneath in minuscule letters: "Sunset on the Sea." That way there's no mistake. Who could have sent me this?

Jacqueline turns it over. Tunisia. She closes her eyes. André is spinning around the armchair in wider and wider circles. Never has the air been so pure, the sun so brilliant; great wafts of life are sweeping it. Even if I am ugly and he's not handsome, my God, at least this will have happened, these few seconds of relief, launched in music, the child, the countryside. . . . I can't even read it with these tears welling up, inexplicable lenses of water distorting my universe.

André retreats, prancing like a circus horse. Noëlle is yelling something, but I can't hear what it is.

This is the most original postcard in this country, and in fact, it's a sunrise, not a sunset.

Send news of tibia. No more room. Take care,
                                Philippe Lipinchky
Relax and Enjoy Camp, Bungalow 83, Row
17, Boukhari
P.S.: The striped suit is not compulsory attire.

"You don't answer me when I ask you to clean
the green beans?"

Jacqueline turns toward Noëlle, who arrives en-
cumbered with pots and casseroles. She stops suddenly.

"What is it? Why are you laughing?"

Jacqueline Puisset hides the card, shaking her
head as her sister sits down at her feet.

I can't get this brilliant smile off my face—it
sticks as though the corners of my lips were rolled
up and glued there like wallpaper.

"I'm not laughing. It's the light, it's so dazzling."

"You are laughing. Good news?"

The bookseller puts her needle aside and takes a
handful of beans.

"Oh, the usual . . . bills . . . you know."

I will write back. That doesn't commit me to anything. Well, I should think about it. . . . I'm always
careful when I hear myself say I should think about
it. Let's not get carried away now.

"What's with you this morning? You don't answer me when I ask you something!"

"Yes, I do. Push the casserole over here."

Noëlle sits down Indian style, facing the burning
sun, and murmurs:

"I should've put oil on."

"Don't worry, you'll get tan."

"Right. So there'll be five of them, because Zelle

is bringing two friends who'll camp on the grass
and . . ."

The singing of the grasshoppers blends in with
her voice; you find them wherever the earth is warm
like this. It's for them that I stay here, for Noëlle,
for the grasshoppers, and because there's no point
in leaving, your problems always go with you. . . .
I'll write this afternoon, when they're all taking their
siestas.

Handfuls of beans patter into the casserole.
Noëlle rattles on incessantly in the glorious sun;
the children run around the hills. Perhaps summer
will never end.

Day after tomorrow will make a week. Not yet
halfway, but almost.

Philippe accelerates uphill. It's better now; at
first I was panting like a seal by the first dune. Eight
miles every morning, interspersed with short sprints.
I've probably already lost five pounds. At least I
won't have come for nothing.

Downhill through the crowds of reclining bodies.
Taking aim, Lipinchky shuts his eyes and heads for
the sea. No obstacles: the sand, the wind, and him
in the middle; a sharp turn, toes in the surf, and
around and back. His heart feels like a gong in his
throat. The sand flies by. There's the camp. What
a pile of . . . Oh well, the nights are calmer now.
Strange as it may seem, the neighbors stop from
time to time. Fatigue, no doubt. The meals are horrible. A designated place between King Kodak with
his pain-ridden wife and Mlle. Flottehue—the muse
of the loom. She weaves everything and anything—
dresses, coats, shawls, shirts. She'll save the world

with her shuttle. Completely whacko! The next table's even worse: two soccer fanatics, one Jehovah's Witness, and an ex-member of the chorus who'll take any pretext to break into *Carmen* at dessert.

The wrestler bursts suddenly into the village and slows down, out of breath. Under the pseudo-arcades the vacationers are hoping for a real breakfast. Philippe sits down.

"You're lucky to be able to run like that," King Kodak's wife whines. "With my eventration and asthma, I can hardly even walk."

She told us that yesterday. She's had two thousand successive operations, her intestines are reinforced throughout with bits of plastic, but there's always a little piece of gut that works its way through the fortifications.

King Kodak plays with his levers and dials and measures the light with the meter he wears around his neck like a religious medal.

"I'll need filters with this light, but with a 2.8, even if I open at 10.5, my depth of field is too short to be focused at infinity."

Philippe nods, vaguely sickened by the sweet chocolate splashing in his cup. It's military chocolate: khaki.

"Asthma's the worst. First it gets you here, starts spreading, and then you've had it. Ask George. Sometimes I practically choke, huh, George?"

George wipes his lens as though polishing the head of a newborn baby.

"Yes, dear."

He couldn't care less. If one day she really does

choke, he'll no doubt photograph the corpse. In color.

"The butter, please."

Philippe turns toward Mlle. Flottehue. Today she's wrapped in a kind of antique-cut cloak. She looks like she's ready to play Phèdre at the matinee at Montargis.

Flottehue leans toward the Queen of Pain.

"Perhaps weaving would help. I've completely cured my ulcers by practicing weaving, you know."

The Queen of Pain twists around.

"Nothing helps, my dear, when it gets you in the kidneys and you're paralyzed to your thighs."

King Kodak dunks his bread, completely indifferent to the problem.

"And you, you don't take pictures?"

Philippe shakes his head. Behind him, the Callas of "Relax and Enjoy" gargles her warmup scales.

"It's always the same thing: overrun the alleys, center holds back, and when it's done they start all over again. It's old hat, there's no spark to it. Those guys are hard-up, whereas Valenciennes in 1957 . . ."

Shrieks of laughter.

"Valenciennes was seventeenth in 1957! You can hardly compare them with Real de Madrid."

> *Love, that rebellious bird,*
> *which none can tame. . . .*

"For my third operation, the surgeon said, 'This time we'll put in a patch; that way it shouldn't come out anymore . . .' "

"Sure, with a telephoto, but have you seen the prices of telephotos? You know how much a telephoto costs? Have you seen the prices? I'm talking about a real telephoto, not some Japanese deal that just looks like one. Well, I'll tell you, a telephoto goes for between . . ."

". . . he just grazed that ball with the side of his foot and angled it into the postage stamp corner, and Duchinois is quite a goalie too . . ."

Philippe yawns. Here's the mail.

"Well, my dear, after two weeks it was open on the left, and do you know why? Because it was too compressed on the right."

I hate eating in the stench of suntan oil. I'd swear it's even on my toast. Oh great, there he is.

Robert-Odilon Trousselier has just emerged, still gurgling:

"Pottery club, acoustic guitar, folk dance, graphic arts. Yours truly, instructor."

Brouhaha . . . the athletic type cruise toward the beach. Water-skiing outboards are already tracing circles in the foam.

"Where's the photography club? Anybody know where the photography club is?"

A panicky King Kodak trots around in circles. Jehovah's Witness heads for the dunes, towel under one arm, Bible under the other.

"Mailman."

Carmen's extended F-sharp fades into the distance.

Hmm, a postcard with grapevines on a hillside. Philippe turns it over. In the left-hand corner: "Grapevines on a Hillside." It's from her.

I'm sending you a card with grapevines on a hillside. Thanks for the sunrise. Tibia recovering nicely. Happy sunbathing. Take care.

"And then, barely three months ago, appendicitis to top it off—and I hadn't even recovered from my last peritonitis and . . ."

"Yuppee!" Philippe murmurs.

Behind him, Carmen stops in mid D-sharp.

"What did you say?"

Philippe stands up, stretches, looks at the sky, Carmen, the Pain Queen, and feels a wave rush through him.

"I said yuppee," he murmurs softly.

They watch him walk toward the bar in the morning light.

"He's funny, that man," Mlle. Flottehue mutters.

The Queen of Pain shudders and leans toward the mezzosoprano.

"Did I tell you they accidentally treated me with X rays? Can you imagine?"

Philippe stops suddenly, frozen in the sunshine.

I'm thirty-seven and a half, and I know she's less walleyed in my imagination than in real life, but I don't give a damn.

I'm getting out of here.

chapter fifteen

PLAYING bocci in a cast may seem like nothing, but in fact it might have been Hercules's thirteenth labor.

Jacqueline extends her arm, masking the hillside with the metal ball.

If I miss, we lose. But if I hit it, we haven't won. It's not fair.

Jacqueline drops her arm.

"Could you move that pebble in front of the little twig, please?"

"Not allowed," says the cousin. "In bocci, you play the field the way it is."

"Give us a break," Noëlle grumbles. "You're leading by four points. The least you could do—"

"No," François says. "Rules are rules."

The women sigh in unison.

They're always on the same team. Noëlle's aim is bad and Jacqueline can't shoot. They always lose, but they never give up.

It's not really the game itself I like but the ritual that goes with it—the glasses on the table, the shadows of the plane trees at the end of the day, the frost from the ice cubes. It's a moment from many years of my life, this ridiculous game along the stones of the old wall.

"Jacqueline, are you playing or making mayonnaise?"

"I'm concentrating. Is that allowed?"

The ball rises to eye level; dazzling rays of sunshine crisscross the metal.

"Someone's at the gate," François says. "I'll go."

"No rush," the cousin sighs, leaning his elbow against the tree, "we'll be here all night."

"Don't bug us," Noëlle says. "You always find some comment to make when it's not your turn."

Jacqueline reaches out her left arm for balance, shuts one eye, leans on her cast, and aims at the *cochonnet,* a minuscule planet light-years in the distance.

"If I get it, that'll be four points."

Noëlle wrings her damp hands into a prayer position that she knows is useless. In all the years she's been playing, her sister has never hit the goal.

"I've got it this time," Jacqueline says.

The ball wavers, the arm gently drops, rises again for one final aim, starts up again—and suddenly there he is with François.

The ball shoots out, a cannonball now, rockets the *cochonnet* thirty yards away, then lands, buried.

Jaws drop in stupefaction; Noëlle jumps into the air; the cousin burns his finger on his match.

My God, somebody pinch me.

"I came by to say hello," Philippe says.

Jacqueline's mouth is still open. It shuts and opens again.

Noëlle is the first to recover.

"Well, that was a good idea. You'll have to stay for dinner, right, Jacqueline?"

"Yes," François says, "stay for dinner."

Jacqueline swallows and clears her throat.

"Yes, stay and have dinner with us," her voice wavers.

"I don't want to impose . . ."

Noëlle jumps up, gathers four balls, drops three of them, throws one right at her cousin still glued to the tree bark.

"Let's get going! You set the table. Oh, that's right, we didn't introduce you: our cousin from Montpellier, this is the man who . . . cracked . . . that is . . . I'll tell you later. Come on François, don't just stand there."

Noëlle drags them off, her matchmaker instincts going strong.

I can hear her whispering from here: "Leave them alone together, he came all the way from Africa just for her." Never an ounce of exaggeration.

My God, he's red! Maybe even redder than I am. Part of it's sunburn, but still . . .

"So, how was Tunisia?"

Philippe clasps his hands behind his back and pushes a pebble around with his toe.

"They tried to make me do folk dances, so I . . ."

Silence.

"I said to myself . . ."

Silence.

"I should just come by and say hello."

Alone. We are alone under the old tree. On the

hill like Pelléas and Mélisande. What we say now
has to count.

"We could sit down."

"No thanks, I was sitting in the car."

He scratches his ear, makes a horrible face, and
adds:

"In fact, I rarely drive standing up."

Jacqueline laughs; he follows. The sentence slides
out by itself without her even thinking about it:

"It was a good idea to come. I'm glad you did.
Can you stay a few days?"

Philippe looks at his watch, then the sky,
scratches his head, and says:

"Yes."

She smiles at him.

"Would you like a drink? I want to hear about
Tunisia."

Suddenly she feels good. A man has come to see
her. What could be more natural? That's allowed,
isn't it? Of course he looks like a pickup truck reared
up on its hind legs, but what of it? He came one
evening, on his own, uncalculating, for the pleasure
of talking, to enjoy the shadows on the hills, the
odor of wild herbs rising with the coming night, the
violet up there invading the crest of the hills. I'd
never noticed it before.

As he attempts to arrange his shoulders on the
narrow back of the chaise longue, something opens
up in him—the peacefulness of the evening. Two
days of panic and hesitation and suddenly everything is so simple.

"It's lovely here," he says softly.

The glass is cold in his hand; the aroma of anise
floats through the air.

No folk dances to worry about.

She's taken the same position as before: almost in profile, the bad eye hidden in the ever-growing purple shadow.

"I'll tell you who's here. You'll get along fine with everyone, you'll see."

I have to tell him he's of the same race as I am. Nothing is easy for people like us, the unattractive ones. It's not exactly with ease that we walk into living rooms. We lack the elegant gestures of those who know that the attention they attract will be admiring. We are different and our chords vibrate painfully, violins of suffering that wince at the slightest touch of the bow. Courage, my frightful wrestler, it'll be tough in a few minutes when you have to go in there: there'll be two of us, of course, but with the combination of our disgraces, we'll have a heavy toll to pay.

"Noëlle and François you know, and if they're not extremely nice, I'll be very angry."

"Okay," Philippe says. "And the little gnat, is he here?"

"There are three of them, but you can still stay. They take off in the morning, come back exhausted, and fall asleep in their chairs at dinner."

"On to the cousin."

"There's also his wife. The Gatineaus. He's in the car business, she's in Social Security. They have a daughter, Zelle, nineteen, who's brought along two admirers, one very limp young man who's training to eat grass, and another who's been trying to make us laugh since he got here."

"That's a lot of people." Philippe sighs.

I have this urge to take his hand again. I must have an enormous tactile protective instinct.

"I don't really like crowds either, but don't worry, it'll work out."

He shifts his feet and scratches his head. He does have nice hair, a nice curly lock. That's not unimportant. It's just afterwards things take a bad turn.

"It's funny," he says, "to have met at the ring and then find ourselves here."

They're quiet for a while. It's the time when the birds veer up high into the sky as it fades, tired from glowing all day long. Nothing is stirring; the valley below wraps up in the first covers of night. Silence.

He crossed the sea for me, just like the lovesick sailors of long ago. He's Ulysses, and little did I know I was Penelope when I was knitting my nephew's sweater. . . . What am I talking about?

"Dinner!"

A far-off voice comes down the path. In the background, the brouhaha of an almost ready meal: children's voices, laughter in the countryside.

"Let's go," Jacqueline says. "When it's time, it's time."

Philippe gets up. He's even more monstrous in the shadows where you can only half-see him. Music suddenly invades the valley. André has turned on the radio.

"Can I help you walk?"

"That's okay, I'm used to it now."

The white cast is the last spot of light rocking through the dying colors, a tiny ghost climbing the path, disappearing, swallowed by the trees.

* * *

Valentin Jolibert, Yoyo for short, one of Zelle's tender admirers, chuckles softly, butters his bread, crunches a radish, and licks the corner of his mouth:

"In fact, then, you never really force it during your matches?"

"Not really."

More chuckling from Yoyo.

The male Gatineau gobbles a shovelful of salad, protesting with a bit of lettuce hanging on his lips:

"And it's a good thing you don't, otherwise there'd be plenty of accidents."

"And who would pay?" Mme. Gatineau injects. "Social Security, that's who."

Yoyo lets out a mouthful of air and looks around with a cunning expression.

"Do you often have accidents?"

"No, it's quite rare."

Lucien Carrier lifts his long transparent hand to wipe a few pieces of field grass from his prophet's beard. In his plate several yellow seeds strike a discordant note in the solid green: Lucien Carrier will eat them later, for dessert.

Noëlle looks at him and mumbles:

"At least put a little oil and vinegar on them."

Lucien lifts his pale face and slowly looks across the table:

"Absolutely not; that way you'll never rediscover the lost contact with the earth."

André dangles his feet in the air, jabs his fork into his steak as though stabbing the duc de Guise, and ejects:

"Why didn't you bring your mask?"

"I didn't think of it, but I'll give you one. I have several."

"And me?" Sebastian, waking up.

"You too."

Patrick is asleep.

"For Patrick too," André says. "Otherwise he'll steal ours."

"Three masks, it's a promise."

Noëlle thanks the new guest with her eyes.

"Anyway, wrestling is completely rigged," Yoyo says. "It's not a sport anymore."

Zelle, who's been nibbling on a crust of bread since the beginning of the meal, shrugs her shoulders.

"Don't be such a pain in the ass, Yoyo."

Cousin Gatineau, her mother, jumps up.

"Can't you think of some other way to express yourself at the dinner table?"

Zelle peers through her bangs.

"Why some other way and why is it particularly at the dinner table that it should be some other way?"

Cousin Gatineau, father, pianos the table.

"Zelle, that'll do."

Zelle opens her mouth to respond. She's wearing an old-fashioned blouse four times too big, army surplus pants from the war of 1870, and at ninety degrees in the shade, is wrapped in seventy pounds of Aztec motifs on a Nicaraguan shawl. From one end emerge her workboots, from the other a forest of reddened, frizzed hair through which we catch an occasional glimpse of a brown eye, round like a marble.

"It's true though, he's a pain in the ass. Don't you think so?"

Mother looks at daughter, grits her teeth, and turns slightly violet.

François begins whistling softly. Jacqueline hands Philippe a bowl.

"Have some more salad."

"So really, if it's rigged," says Yoyo, "we could all be wrestlers. Do you like wrestling?"

"It's my profession," Philippe says gently. "Sometimes I like it, sometimes it bores me."

"It's like cars," says Cousin Gatineau. "Sometimes it's . . . and then other times it's . . . it's impossible: I walk in front of a garage and I get hives."

"That's like me at Social Security."

Snickering from Yoyo. Lucien chews his grass.

"Yes, young man, maybe that makes you laugh, but I do work for Social Security. At least I work. And you, can you tell me what you do?"

"Okay, Mom, it's decided, once and for all, he's a pain in the ass," Zelle says.

"When do I get my mask?"

"As soon as I go home, I'll send it."

"Is it true," Yoyo says, "that there are women completely naked under their coats who wait for you after the match?"

Noëlle jumps as though she'd sat on a loose spring.

"François, put the children to bed please."

"No, I don't wanna go to bed," André says. "Why are the ladies naked?"

"Let's go," Jacqueline injects. "Come with me, off to bed."

"Personally," says Philippe, "I've never seen any."

Lucien Carrier delicately samples his first golden seed.

"Hey, why are they naked? What's your name?"

"Philippe. Because they're too warm."

"Get going," François says. "You ask too many questions."

"You're a pain in the ass," Zelle says.

"André, tell everyone good night. You too, wave good night."

"Give 'em a break, Noëlle," Zelle says. "They'll say good night when they want to say good night."

"Good night to everyone except Zelle 'cause she's a pain in the ass," André says.

"This child gets more and more difficult," Noëlle says dreamily. "What are we going to do with him, François?"

François picks up the yawning child and carries him off.

Cousin Gatineau looks at her daughter's hair and wonders if she'd recognize her in the street with her face exposed.

"Do you think you'll ever go to the hairdresser's or are you going to spend your entire life behind that curtain?"

"Come on," Jacqueline intervenes. "Worry about that later. Pass the cheese over here and leave your daughter alone for a few minutes."

Philippe swallows his last french fries, wonders what he could possibly say, and finds nothing. Next to him, Carrier chomps on his summer flowers.

The tall chimney rises to the beamed ceiling; dispersed on the red tile floor are colored blocks, tin soldiers, plastic trucks.

"Do you like it?" asks Noëlle, following the path of his eyes.

"Yes, it's . . . it's difficult to explain, but it seems comfortable, pleasant to live in."

How idiotic. I've got to work on this. My brain muscles just aren't developed enough to make speeches.

"Here, it's not rigged," Yoyo sneers.

This guy is looking for trouble. I can feel it. I know that slippery wise-guy look. What he'd like is to make me tremble. He wants to feel tough. In short, a wretched little ass.

François comes back down the waxed wooden stairs.

"Two are snoring. André's almost asleep and sends you a special good night."

Philippe blushes, flattered.

"He's sure to become your biggest fan," Jacqueline says. . . . Well, that's good anyway, since this Yoyo is definitely trying to make trouble. Philippe's ill at ease, but he doesn't really dare put him in his place, and I can't do it for him. There he goes; it's starting up again.

"By the way," Yoyo says.

Jacqueline gets up.

"Who wants coffee?"

Noëlle jumps.

"Sit down, crazy legs, I'll do it. Now, who wants some?"

Philippe refuses. Yoyo is relentless:

"In fact, it's a profession you can practice a long time since you don't have to make much of an effort. What age will you retire at?"

He's bugging me, he's really bugging me.

"Listen, if you're really interested, I can sign you up with a club, you'll find out all about it. But I'm warning you, the training is tough."

Carrier silently leaves the table and assumes the lotus position on the tiles, facing the open door, looking out into the night. I wonder if he's going to chew his cud now.

Beaming from ear to ear, François gets out the bottle of old cognac. For him it's the best moment, when that peaceful feeling settles in. Noëlle, Jacqueline, and the cousin clear the table.

Summer nights. Like old times. Zelle wraps up in her shawl until she's no more than a ball of fur by the fireplace. Gatineau sniffs his glass and compares it with last year's—fruitier, but not so strong.

The voices fade. A soft freshness from the valley infiltrates the atmosphere.

I didn't say very much. She's gonna take me for a real idiot, if she hasn't already. . . . My head is completely empty. I've lived alone so long I've completely lost the touch for conversation. I've settled little by little into my silence.

A perfumed, burning-white sensation punctures his tear duct. Yoyo giggles when he sees the wrestler's eyes water under the brutal assault of the alcohol.

"Not like in the ring, huh? That's the real thing, not make-believe this time."

The limit has been passed.

He has put his big, arrogant toe over a perilous frontier. If I let him get away with this, I've had it.

Philippe Lipinchky gets up, scratches his head, perplexed, and turns toward François.

"Do you have a phone book?"

Surprised, François Louberan looks at his guest.
"Yes. You want to call someone at this hour?"
"No, I'd just like the phone book."

This time it's me they're looking at. Yoyo seems to have decided to shut his big mouth. He is obviously intrigued. Even the Buddhist is coming out of his meditation. As for the bookseller, she hasn't missed a word.

Noëlle comes back into the light of the lamp.
"Here you are."

Philippe takes it, leafs through the pages. There are 450.

"Do you have another one?"
"Which one?"
"Doesn't matter."

Total silence. This time Gatineau brings the second.

"It's the Charente-Maritime one. Is that okay?"
"Fine."

Philippe puts the two books on top of one another, 832 pages in all, and stands in front of Yoyo.

Zelle looks out from between her bangs.

"Of course it's rigged," Philippe says, "but it's not all that easy to do. You have to work at it, to train, practice. And then, from time to time, you get somebody who really wants to win, or who loses his cool, nervous types, and then you gotta hold 'em back."

Peals of laughter, with a wagonload of mockery.

"Very funny," Yoyo says.

"I'll show you one of our tricks," Philippe says. "Imagine this is your neck."

Jacqueline watches the right tricep inflate the shirt. The arms are extended, the legs set wide, and the hips suddenly pivot. A shadow in the lamplight, the torso fills the room. Breathless, she watches: the mass of pages is sliced in two equal parts, as though with a saw.

Philippe puts them on the bare table and sits back down, untouchable. He knows he's won, and that Yoyo, if he keeps laughing, won't laugh so hard.

François and Cousin Gatineau whistle in unison.

The women stare at Philippe.

"Will you have another little drop, Monsieur Philippe?" chimes Noëlle.

Philippe turns around and smiles. He looks like the Rock of Gibraltar at its calmest possible moment. He and Jacqueline exchange glances.

"I'd like it if you'd call me Philippe," he says.

The silence of trees and hillsides. A night like so many, warm and silky, rubbing against the smooth stones and tangled grasses.

Jacqueline feels a peaceful river flow through her veins in the light of the moon. For once I bring home a man and they certainly can't say he's like everyone else. The wooden table feels smooth and polished under her palms.

"I propose a game of gin rummy. Do you play, Philippe?"

Behind them, the Buddhist has resumed his position, facing the moon.

chapter sixteen

THE shining olives slide into the tomato juice.

"Do you have anchovies, Noëlle?"

"In the cupboard, on the top shelf."

Jacqueline clomps toward the back of the large kitchen. The sun is burning through the window panes. She stops and pushes her hair back with her fist so as not to touch it with her oily hand.

Cries explode from the back of the garden.

"They're still torturing him," Jacqueline says.

Noëlle takes the eggs off the stove. The water is still boiling.

"That reminds me, I wanted to talk to you about something."

Bad sign. When Noëlle says, "I wanted to talk to you about something," that something is not pleasant to talk about.

Jacqueline sits down in front of the fennels, knife in hand. She loves making those summer salads everyone's crazy about.

"Go ahead, I'm listening."

"It's about Philippe."

The knife pierces the hard white flesh and the perfume rises in successive spirals.

"Do you think he came this far to teach your nephews Greco-Roman?"

Zelle comes in, sniffs, and drags her rubber soles into the other room, arms buried under a cape the color of a gravestone. Her hair resembles a thatched roof sliding lugubriously down her skull.

"I see you don't need my help. See you later."

"The good thing when you talk," Noëlle says, "is that then we know which is the front and which is the back. What have you done with your young hopefuls?"

Zelle stops, raises her arms to heaven.

"Lucien's in the pasture, Yoyo must still be asleep."

"Not even eleven thirty," Noëlle chuckles. "It's his age. The little one's not too resilient. He needs his sleep."

Jacqueline gets up, joining Zelle at the doorway.

"Will you please set the table? Everyone gets to work a little."

Zelle doesn't budge, just watches through her protective veil as Jacqueline goes off toward the garden.

"What's wrong with her?" she asks. "She seems pissed off."

Noëlle cuts the last egg and disperses it in the varnished pottery bowl.

"What do you expect?" she says. "It's love. It gets us all one day, but when it comes late, it's even worse."

As fast as the cast permits, Jacqueline hobbles down the path with ten thousand warriors at her heels. There he is.

"Philippe!"

He gets up, two children attached to his legs, a third on his shoulders.

"Can you take me to the village? I forgot the onions."

Philippe looks at her, surprised.

"There're lots of them in the basement."

"Okay," Jacqueline says. "If you'd rather stay and play, that's your privilege. I'll go down with François."

Half choking, Philippe stammers:

"B-b-but I didn't say no. . . . Okay, let's go."

"We wanna go too," André says.

"No, we don't need you. You stay here."

Stunned, the three children stare at their aunt. Usually she brings cakes, plays cars, knits sweaters with pockets full of candy. Patrick reacts first:

"You're a pain in the ass, Tata."

Jacqueline lifts up her cast and sticks it under the glove compartment. She fastens her seat belt. Philippe shuts her door and gets in behind the wheel. She rolls down her window as the motor roars and leans toward her nephews.

"You guys are a triple pain in the ass!"

As they wind down the twisting road, the trees thin out and then come the red-clay terraces. We haven't been alone since he arrived.

Philippe watches her out of the corner of his eye: something is wrong. He downshifts and lets the car glide, honking at each bend.

"What is it?"

Jacqueline bites the nail of her index finger. Ever since he came I've been biting my fingernails. I was perfectly happy. I like my profession, I've got the second-floor room to organize, there's the town; why look for something more? Then comes Philippe, this enormous bulk, like a dead weight. We've got to stop so I can get hold of myself and just tell him bluntly, honestly, that neither of us is fifteen years old anymore.

"My sister drives me crazy. She's never gotten used to the idea that I can live alone. She sees you arrive and she starts building castles in Spain."

I said it.

It's clear this way. It's better.

Philippe veers to the left, in line with the view. At the edge of the plain you can see the stones of a castle in ruins.

"Listen, it's good that we talk about it. We can stop a minute."

The wind is strange here. Nothing stops it. Jacqueline pulls up a reed and goes to lean against the parapet, eyes closed against the violent gusts.

He's near her and his hair is flying. In five years it'll all be gray, the temples, on top . . .

"There's a lot of wind," he says.

It's true it's not going to be easy, but I'm the one who wanted this explanation.

The grasses on the slope lie down, crushed by an invisible, all-powerful hand.

"I have my life, Philippe—a town, a profession, a family, my habits . . . I . . . I like you very much, but there's one thing I know for sure, and that is that I don't want to change anything. It's awkward telling you this because I don't even know if you intended . . ."

He sits down and tries desperately to light a cigarette in the shelter of his hands. Normally, he smokes only two a day, after lunch and dinner.

She's right. I shouldn't get carried away. I've got my friends, my neighborhood, the training, the matches. . . . Where does she fit into all that? We each have complete worlds with no room for . . .

"I like you a lot too, and I think we get along well, but, well, I don't want to change anything either. And we're really different, but, well . . . I think if I were twenty years old it might be different."

She's sitting near him. The reed dances crazily on her lips.

"I wasn't very pretty at twenty either, as you can imagine."

The tobacco sizzles each time he inhales, a minuscule noise perceptible even in the bellowing that fills the plains.

"But nice curves," Philippe says. "That counts."

A bitter tenderness. Autumn isn't so far off after all. I hadn't noticed it all these days, but today it's different. There's something in the color of the trees that feels like the death of summer, an aging, a usury in the splendor of the unfurling countryside. Already the sky is no longer the same as in the postcards—two postcards that have changed everything. Two rectangles of cardboard with exaggerated colors, with words that don't count—and suddenly a stronger dose of life arrives with new tints, new . . .

"It bothers me that Noëlle thought that," Philippe

says. "You must have been ill at ease these last few days."

Now everything's getting mixed up. There's his hand, crushing out his cigarette on the hot stones, that hand I touched with my hand before. I've got to either say something or cry. . . .

"Everything's happened so quickly in four days."

In the movies they look at each other with tenderness, assured, confident. For us, well, we do our best.

"Maybe it's better not to talk so much," Philippe says. "It's really the first time and it doesn't seem to make us very happy."

A chill runs through her. The warmth of the sun is diluted by the furious gusts.

They go back to the car, surprised by the sudden silence.

"So, that's that," Philippe says.

He looks over. She's looking straight ahead.

It's not easy to love someone—gotta have the physique. So, do it like in the movies, go for it. You don't care if she doesn't look like Rita Hayworth. You wanna do it, so do it! "I don't want to change anything." What kind of bullshit is that? When you go home at night, is it always nice and cheerful, your little dinner in front of the window? And the watercolors in the afternoon, all alone, chasing those nuances with that stupid little brush? That's what you don't want to change? Tell her you lied, that in fact, you'd like to tear it all up, and she would too; she must. Shit, you can tell she's had it to here with her bland life. Just look at her, damn it! If that jerk Dantron were here, it'd already be taken care of, seats folded down and on with the big maneuvers.

All women want it, all men too, so I don't see what's
so difficult. I've just gotta go for it. I'll stop on a side-
road and it'll work out fine . . . well, maybe not . . .
that is, she doesn't really seem to be the type. And,
for that matter, neither am I. Also, even if all women
want it, they don't all want it all the time, and maybe
she doesn't want it today. What's more, not only do
they not all want it all the time, they don't all want
it with just anybody. So she might not only not want
it today, she might not want it with me; so with one
thing aggravating another, chances are good that I'll
blow the whole thing. Plus, at forty, or almost, I'm
not gonna throw myself on her like a madman. What
if I scare her and she screams, or if I break her other
leg? Wrestler and rapist, that's all I need.

"Anyway, I've got to leave tomorrow—I have to
be in Aubervilliers on Saturday."

The castle fades in the distance, a mural buffeted
by the wind.

"It's gone by quickly," she sighs.

They say nothing more.

He's not moving. A block of granite. I was a
little tough, a little too direct. A cold shower. I always get carried away . . . and then regret it. And
with this damned gearshift, no way to do the knee
bit. Now what kind of thought is that? Anyway,
doing the knee bit with one leg in plaster might
turn into an acrobatic performance. If I had normal
eyes, I could try what they call "the meaningful
look." Out of the question.

I wonder if the seats recline. Jacqueline, think
about something else. It's not healthy, as your sister
would say.

What would happen if I touched him? First of all,

we'd skid out of control, and then . . . I don't know if he really likes me. We're good pals, but he's never tried anything with me. Right now he could. This would be the ideal moment. God knows what he's thinking about, but it's surely not the same thing I am! Come on, get a hold of yourself.

It's settled now—no pain, no complications. But it's funny how, more and more each year, summer goes by so quickly.

chapter seventeen

I WAS embarrassed. That's what really counts in the end: ashamed, in respect to Noëlle, François, the Gatineaus and their cocker spaniel of a daughter, even the kids, everybody.

Jacqueline puts down her pen.

Arsène Vandelier-Ménole has just risen at the other end of the room. To say he has risen is not quite accurate, as there is a curious phenomenon that occurs each time Arsène stands up: he is shorter than when sitting.

Thus he is the only person in the world who in order to stand up, should sit down.

Anyway you put it, he is not tall.

Not a dwarf; probably the category just above.

My God, it's hot in this room! There are at least three thousand of us. Well, let's say a hundred and leave it at that.

I'm bored. I feel like going outside. There's nothing worse than being shut up in a convention. The weather is splendid for this time of year, and I'm stuck here, nailed to my seat. There are still lots of leaves on the trees on the Champs-Élysées; I saw them as I went by in the taxi. Everything is golden, from the Arc de Triomphe to the Obélisque, with a crisp breeze fluttering the pages of the magazines in the kiosks. A blue sky from the Sacré-Coeur to the Tour Montparnasse. I've got to buy a pair of jeans, and sunglasses, since I forgot mine. That, plus some irresistibly chic top, and Paris, look out!

"It is certain that we cannot always be counselors for our customers. Do we even have the right to be? Can we assume to know what suits them? But the woman who comes in to buy *Le Père Goriot,* can we let her leave with *Emmanuelle*?"

Oh shut up, Arsène, you get on my nerves. Barely three o'clock. The Champs-Élysées in the sunshine, rue Saint-Honoré, rue de la Paix, the banks of the Seine . . . a little movie theater in the Latin quarter. . . . I've wanted to take this trip for a long time without even knowing it. It hit me like a cannonball.

After all, it's not often I treat myself to a little fantasy, and I've worked my head off since vacation. I deserve to go a little crazy for forty-eight hours. Although with Arsène the folly is pretty limited, if not nonexistent.

Jacqueline rolls her eyes toward heaven, that is, toward the ceiling.

Huge hotel conference room. Meeting place for multiple conventions. Today the booksellers, tomorrow the information engineers, the next day the retired railroad officials. I've had it to here with these conventions!

What if I pretend to go to the ladies' room? Once in the hall, I could make my escape.

"To attract the customer and not lose him, expansion and retention, these are the two axes on which we should base our work, because I believe this is the moment to say it . . ."

If we get out around six all the stores will be closed, night will fall, and there goes my outing. . . .

Jacqueline leans toward her neighbor, whose eyes shut regularly every ten seconds. Her lips brush against the ear.

"At what time is the session over?"

With a superhuman effort the woman turns her glaucous eyes toward Jacqueline. You'd think she was dragging an invisible tractor.

"Around five thirty, but there's a reception with wine afterwards."

Catastrophe! I'll bet anything we're going to be treated to mousseux. Mousseux and dry biscuits, like with Odette. It's the standard six o'clock fare. I should have known. Okay, get a hold of yourself, my dear, you're a responsible adult, you do what you want, and you're going to just get up quietly and head for the door. You have your rights, after all.

Another yawn is stifled behind her.

"Who among us is not aware that a book has nothing to do with a can of peas or a bottle of rosé de Provence? Because, you see . . ."

Maybe it's because of my eye, but I feel like Arsène is talking specifically to me.

"Excuse me."

Jacqueline stands up, purse stashed under her arm, and advances crablike through the cramped knees. Men stand up; brouhaha of chairs.

Incredible. I had hardly decided and suddenly I

was up, bag under one arm, raincoat under the other. When they see I don't come back it's going to look terrible!

Jacqueline Puisset races down the stairway, is hit by an enormous ray of sun, and stops at the threshold of the building.

The people in the street grimace under the intense light and seem to be smiling at me. *J'adore Paris!*

The bookseller strikes out, heading for the boulevard. The city unfolds around her, golden and glittering, shop windows reflected and reflecting. When I think of those poor people up there listening to Arsène. . . . He'll be at it for two days now. They'll be there at the end of the week, dead from exposure, and I'll be cruising around the capital. You only live once, and I'm not going to wait until I'm ninety to go on a shopping spree.

Tapered mannequins with bald heads and doe eyes, wrapped in ephemeral netting and scarves . . . psychedelic music, revolving spotlight: the aquarium atmosphere. That outfit's not bad; with a pair of scissors and a flour sack you could probably do as well, provided you used only one hand.

The grenadine carpets turn apricot under the morbid lighting. I'm wandering through a gleaming Amazonian jungle, between velvet vines . . . only thing missing's the crocodiles. A boutique like that in Perpignan and you'd have a collective suicide.

Piled high in a huge laundry basket is an assortment of artistically unraveled T-shirts. Jacqueline digs through. With this light it's hard to know if it's dusty rose, smoked salmon, crushed strawberry, lemon yellow, or pistachio green. No, it's not for

my age, it's more for Zelle, if she ever decides to
take off her poncho.

"Do you have jeans?"

The saleswoman turns around. She weighs maybe
eighty pounds, Eurasian, in gold shorts, copper belt,
thigh-high suede boots, apple-green leotard, and
chrome-framed motorcycle goggles.

"We don't do jeans."

Extraordinary voice. She could sing *Boris Godu-
nov*.

Jacqueline emerges into the fresh air and the
crowd.

The Opéra isn't far. I'll go up the avenue.

Jacqueline climbs the avenue in the dust of the
Indian summer, and little by little her wild enthusiasm melts. Signs in travel agencies: India for two
weeks, weekend in Canada, Four-day Safari . . . as
though all of Paris were trying to escape from Paris
. . . Tokyo, Montreal, the Philippines. She sees herself walking, reflected in the windows and stainless
steel. I wonder if I don't look too much like the
provinces. My left heel is starting to rub—one more
block and I'll have a blister like a lightbulb—at least
one hundred twenty watts.

What a monument, the Opéra! A big round box
with a green-gray lid. Pick it up and it sings, full
blast. My feet hurt; hurry, it's green.

Race in the crosswalk. The crowd is thick now.
In the trembling, dusty light, she makes out the
facade of the Galeries Lafayette. If I don't find it
here, I'll never find it. My toes are making sparks.

Jacqueline dives through the revolving door and
stops, taken aback. A gigantic sign floats over the
counters. SALE!! A hundred thousand women tear-

ing at each other. She takes a deep breath and charges into the melee.

Plaouf!
As they say in high society.

A woman has just collapsed in a chair on the terrace of a big corner café. If she takes up only one chair, her packages take up two more.

"A beer on tap, please."

The waiter glances at the bags surrounding the customer-avalanche and wonders if any creature having only two arms could possibly transport all that without assistance, then walks lazily off toward the bar.

"One draught on the terrace."

The customer is wearing a shirt with scenes depicting the Scandinavian plains and a prefaded, double stitched, Italian rivet-pocket, back-buckled, big belt-looped, zipper-closed, 100 percent stabilized cotton, western form, unshrinkable, machine washable, no-iron pair of jeans. I had a hard time finding this damned pair of jeans.

To complete the picture, I treated myself to a fabulous pair of clogs—natural leather uppers, elastomere sole, wooden heel, design across the top. In short, only in Paris can you find such a marvel. Of course, when I come down the stairs, you'd think it was the second armored division, but I needed them—my toes were like marmalade and my heels at a hundred twenty degrees Fahrenheit.

"Thank you."

Jacqueline sinks her lips into the cold, bitter foam. It's so good! Paris is ravishing again. But what a battle to get up to the counters! I got the same

jeans for Noëlle, two or three things for the kids: a
sailor's sweater for André, with raglan sleeves,
rounded pockets, and reinforced elbows. It'll be
good for winter. And then some striped socks, a
little sweater that was really a bargain, a scarf, suntan oil, colored towels, a set of casseroles I've
wanted for twenty years, and various other knick-
knacks, not to mention what's on my nose: deep-sea
diver style smoked sunglasses—the perfect compro-
mise between a gas mask and granny glasses.
Decked out the way I am now—blue jeans, clogs,
the eye safe behind my shades—I'm quite the swinging chick.

What am I going to do tonight? A movie before
going back to the hotel, or maybe I should call a
friend. . . .

The beer is just the way I like it. It's fattening,
but I'm not at that point yet. These clogs are fantastic!

I think I'll call. It'll be good for me to talk to
someone. Let's see, who could I call among my
many admirers? Well, there's 828-13-03, for example. That'll do as well as any, I suppose. Why not?

It's cool inside the café. Jacqueline clomps in.

"A *jeton,* please."

"Downstairs to the right."

Ball-point pen graffiti above the pile of phone
books—you name it, from declaration of love to
winged penises. *Young man looking for partner to
make* . . . It's erased. I wonder what it is he wants
to make; something tells me it isn't crepes.

My heart is shaking the phone booth. It's ridiculous. I succeeded in not thinking about this evening
all day, and now, at the last minute, I'm a wreck. So

what? I come to Paris, I call a friend just to say hello, it's completely innocent, what's the big deal? Anyway, I'm sure he won't be there, and I don't want to go to bed too late because . . .

A voice rough as an old board jumps against her ear.

"Hello, Léon Cro-Magnon here."

Incredible, the telephone. You call from a café on the Grands Boulevards and the Neanderthal Man answers. Direct line to the prehistoric.

"I'd like to speak to Monsieur Lipinchky please."

"Hold on, just a minute."

Strange background noises. Dull blows, yelling, echoes. I wonder if . . .

"Hello, yes?"

Still Cary Grant's voice. When you see him it's a little disappointing, but to hear him, you have to admit it's pleasant.

"Philippe? Jacqueline here."

Silence. I bet he's going to ask Jacqueline who. I'll just bet.

Sudden gasp.

"Well, I'll be . . . but, where are you?"

Lost the bet.

"Here in Paris. I came for a booksellers' convention and . . ."

"Well, I'll be . . . that's . . . that's great, that's really great. So, can we see each other?"

"Yes, well, I'm only free tonight because tomorrow I leave and . . ."

"Well, I can't get over it. Where are you exactly?"

"In a café. I just did a little shopping and . . ."

"I'm coming. I'll be there in a minute and we can have dinner together, okay?"

"Fine. I'm even hungry."

"I'll jump in the métro and be there in . . ."

"I don't want to bother you if you're busy. I . . ."

"Not at all. Léon and I were just working out with some youngsters. How are you anyway?"

"Fine, just fine. And you?"

"Oh, I'm fine. How d'you like this weather? You'd think you're in Perpignan."

"It's true, I feel right at home."

"And the little varmints, they okay?"

"Just fine. André always talks about you. He was thrilled with his mask. It was nice of you to remember."

"Well, I promised."

Jacqueline jumps. An index finger is violently pounding the glass.

"There's someone waiting. I've got to hang up. See you in a minute, okay?"

Anguished yelling.

"The address! You didn't give me the address!"

"It's—I don't know the name of the café. It's on the Boulevards, there's a terrace . . ."

"There are three hundred thousand cafés with a terrace on the Boulevards, you know."

"Wait a minute."

Jacqueline opens the door. The irascible is there, combination Argentine tango dancer and sleazy lawyer.

"Do you know the name of this café?"

Rudolph Valentino looks at her as though she'd just disembarked from a flying saucer.

"The Balto," he says.

Jacqueline shuts the door.

"Whew," Philippe says, "that scared me. I'll be really happy to see you."

"Me too, I'll be very happy . . ."

"Especially," he says, "since I was afraid there might have been a little misunderstanding between us."

"What misunderstanding?"

"Oh well, you know . . ."

The door shakes. This imbecile's going to break the glass knocking like that.

"I'm sorry, but there's someone pounding on the door. See you in a minute."

Jacqueline walks out, very dignified, as Rudolph Valentino hurries in to hide a bomb in the booth.

I am happy.

chapter eighteen

I ALMOST walked right past without recognizing her, she's so splendid.

"And Yoyo, have you seen him since?"

"Apparently he's training to tear up phone books."

She laughs.

"No, in fact, I haven't seen him. I suppose his pal is getting ready to spend the winter in a stable."

When it comes to doing a little shopping, she doesn't kid around. She won't have come for nothing. It's funny to see her here where I live. She exports well. There are those who don't stand up to the change; they're just fine in their own decor, but when they change surroundings, they fade, completely lost, like cut flowers when you dump the water.

Philippe Lipinchky sips his beer slowly, making it last, and tries not to be too surprised by his reflection in the side windows. It's tough to admit that

seeing your own reflection will always be an unpleasant surprise. . . . She's in great shape.

"It's funny to see you without the cast."

I shouldn't have had two beers. I'm going to be
drunk and that won't make a very good impression.
What am I after anyway? I'm happy he's here, but
where does that get us? His tie is horrible—a sunset
melting into fireworks.

"So how is work going?"

"So so. I had a match at Rueil Sunday, and some
guy got worked up and threw a beer bottle from
about ten feet."

Jacqueline leans over: there's a mauve line near
the arch of his eyebrow. She touches it lightly with
her finger.

"Does it still hurt?"

The second time I've touched him. That'll give
me something to dream about for the next fifteen
years.

"We'll have to have a look around Paris," he
says. "For once you're here, so you're not gonna
miss out on that. I'm gonna show you everything."

"The problem is this," she says, pointing to the
mountain of packages surrounding her.

"Doesn't matter, you'll see."

Philippe gathers the packages in one hand, sticks
the casseroles under his arm, and gets up.

I'm not always undesirable.

There are moments when, depending on the lighting, my mood, my state of mind, I tell myself, after
all, there are those shaped more strangely than I am.

Here in the piercing, almost horizontal rays inun-
dating the Boulevards, I am splendid and robust.
She drains her glass quickly—the golden beer swells

her turned-up throat. She's great, too, damn it! You have to admit it, you have to believe it.

The coins clink on the marble.

"The Eiffel Tower," he says. "That's where we start, but we'll have to push it if we want to get there before the sunset."

Jacqueline laughs and breaks into a trot to follow him.

"But I've seen the Eiffel Tower, it's horrible."

"Exactly, but you have to experiment a little."

"Don't run so fast. How will we get there?"

"Métro. Six ten, it's the perfect time, you'll see. I've got tickets in my right-hand pocket; take two, my hands are full."

Jacqueline gallops up, digs into his pocket, finds the tickets, dodges the crowd, gets four elbow jabs in the ribs, clomps down twelve steps.

"Wait for me."

Philippe charges in. I can't believe the racket these clogs make.

The underground odor grabs Jacqueline in the throat. It's at least ninety degrees in here: an enormous unwashed armpit.

If I don't hang on to him, I'll lose him for sure.

Between the heads Philippe ejects:

"We get off at Trocadéro."

Here's the train.

There are at least a billion per car, glued to the windows. Chaos breaks loose when the doors open and the tide pours out. My God, my feet are no longer touching, and I'm still going forward.

Nose in the wrestler's shoulder blades, Jacqueline slowly suffocates, standing on one foot as an elbow penetrates her ear.

"Once it gets to be rush hour," Philippe whispers from the corner of his mouth, "they really pack 'em in. In fact, tonight there're fewer folks than usual."

"Hompf!" says Jacqueline.

Trocadéro.

Groggy, she pops out like a champagne cork, she and a million other passengers.

"Quite a change from Perpignan, huh?"

Sadistic, this guy, no pity whatsoever.

Deafened by the racket, she climbs the last steps into a sudden flood of light. The esplanade—an immense plane of marble tiles, innumerable bridges, golden statues, and slow stairways. The Seine below like an unfurled ribbon, and at the foot of the bridge, the limestone horses, petrified in mid-kick, their manes eternally blown by the absent wind.

She blinks, dizzy in the intense light, the way a traveler staggers on the deck of a boat, intoxicated by the sea.

Philippe points his loaded-down arm.

"That's the Cité over there—those two islands."

He says that as though navigating the South Pacific, between coral reefs.

"It's beautiful. Shall we go down?"

They walk down among the statues, into the park with huge old trees and fountains shimmering in the last rays of sun over the blue basins.

There are two of us, and that has never happened to me. I am more than happy I came. Those people up there with Arsène, if they could see me now . . .

"What's that over there? The big monument with the columns on the right."

He scratches his head.

"If I were a liar, I'd tell you it's the Académie

Française, but frankly, I have no idea. You know, this isn't my neighborhood."

"Where is your neighborhood?"

"It's near Montmartre. Would you like to see it?"

"Yes, but let's take a taxi. One asphyxiation per day is enough."

He puts down the packages and slaps his forehead.

"We'll walk around up there and then go eat at Little Louis's. He's a friend of mine. It's comfortable, you eat well; that is, it's not the Négresco, but I think you'll like it."

He's all excited—sometimes it seems like he's twelve years old, Mephisto. He scans the avenue, then takes off in a hundred-meter dash.

The taxi slows down in front of him.

They collapse into the back among the packages.

"Rue Tholozé . . . not too out of breath?"

They pass the low walls along the river. Notre-Dame over there, and the Louvre, pearl-gray in the hollow of the vermilion gardens of dusk. Here I am, Jacqueline Puisset, spinning through Paris, a merry-go-round of streets and palaces from long ago, the music of . . .

Resting her neck on the back of the seat, she closes her eyes. Philippe smiles, the casseroles on his lap. Darkness will never come again.

chapter nineteen

SHE stands there stupefied, watching him create.

The cream swirls into smooth white peaks crushed under the liquid cataract of chocolate. Three flips of the wrist and it's mixed. He stashes it in the fridge.

"One chocolate mousse coming up."

She crosses her arms, severe.

"When I think you told us you didn't know how to cook!"

Unperturbed, he hooks a spaghetti on the prong of the fork, inhales, bites the noodle, and cuts the gas.

"That's because I do it too well. I'd have spent my whole vacation in front of the stove."

She sips her martini and zeroes in on his portfolios.

"Can I look?"

Funny to see her here. To say the least. I always

forget Little Louis's is closed on Tuesdays. I hope
she doesn't think I did it on purpose to get her up
here. Machiavelli plus Casanova, that's too much.

In any case, she didn't seem to mind coming up—
in bare feet too. With clogs tromping over her head,
Madame Vignoux would never find the sound sleep
she's been after for seventy years.

Makes me nervous having all my painting exposed like that. Shit, my velouté de génisse à la
Marie-Louise!

Philippe opens the oven, splashes with white
wine, and turns down the temperature.

"If I'd had some anchovies," he says, "I'd have
made you a veal à la Montmorency. By the way, do
you like cheese?"

"Reasonably well."

He rubs his hands together, adds some tomato
concentrate to his sauce, a dash of coriander, a little
oregano, and a pinch of saffron.

"I'm gonna make you a cheese cocktail with some
Saint-Nectaire. I'm the only one in the world who
can fix you that."

"Who's this?"

Philippe looks at the portrait on the dresser: a
dignified Victoria Lipinchky, standing proud, leaning on a parasol the size of a beach umbrella. Behind her, a painted cloth rose garden is lost in a
trompe l'oeil perspective. The snapshot has taken
on the faded pink tints of an old-fashioned nursery.

"My mother. I go see her as much as I can. She
would have liked me to be a lawyer and family man,
but she has to settle for a bachelor wrestler."

Jacqueline smiles and sniffs.

"Something smells good. What have you got sizzling in there? For me, it's a real occasion if my omelette turns out."

"An omelette is a lot trickier than most people think—don't speak too lightly of it. It's too bad I don't have time to fix you a Florentine special; then you'd see what a mixture of shrimp, blueberry jam, and smoked lard can do."

She tilts her head up to study the geraniums, like the Japanese in the Louvre. She examines them with something less than admiration.

"Of course, next to the *Radeau de la Méduse*," he says, "it doesn't really stand up, but, well, to each his own."

"I like it though. The petals are perhaps a weak point, but . . ."

"The guy who answered the phone, Léon Cro-Magnon, thinks it's the leaves that are bad."

He studies it, perplexed, and adds:

"Personally, I think the stem is quite good, don't you?"

She laughs.

"Yes. I'm hungry."

"We'll start with the spaghetti Bolognèse."

"I'll set the table."

I don't know why I thought about Fabienne just now. She's so naturally beautiful that I've often wondered if, with a natural air, I wouldn't be beautiful too. It doesn't work—I've seen myself in mirrors. When I try to look natural, I look like a preposterous aristocrat sipping a putrid poison from a filthy cup. To be Fabienne tonight, just tonight, just right now. . . . I'd leave at midnight, like Cinderella. She'd be perfect if she were here, eyeliner, mascara, blue-shadowed lid. Life is so easy for her;

she doesn't have to sit at just the right angle. At forty I'm confronting people in profile, like an Egyptian dancer. There're probably people I know who have never seen my right side. I could have half a moustache and they wouldn't even know. My hands are sweaty.

She sets the glasses on the waxed cloth; he opens the frosty bottle of rosé de Provence.

"I'll serve."

The pasta is steaming through a rusty sauce—colors from the carcasses of sunken ships, deserted dockyards.

"It's really good."

The cold wine excites Jacqueline's appetite. She digs in with enthusiasm.

"I'm ravenous tonight. What a day!"

He laughs, watching her devour the firm pasta, gets up, and brings out the soup.

"Taste this for me."

Satisfied by the first helping, she leans back in her chair.

He's looking at my bad eye. An eye can be crazy just like a brain. Why not? Sometimes I've wondered. It's stupid, but I've often thought about it, just shutting that eye forever. One-eyed to be beauful that is, less ugly, less comic. It is comic being walleyed. Forty years of making people laugh—it gets old. Tonight it's worse than ever; tonight I'd give anything, I'd give years of my life, if the wanderer would just stay put . . .

Philippe puts the serving dish on the table and sits down gently, dish towel in hand.

He purrs:

"It's impossible to have an operation?"

She shakes her head, shedding a tear onto the tablecloth, a perfect circle, trembling and irregular only on the liquid edges riding the red and white checks.

If only it had been, my dear man, if only it had been . . .

"It's ridiculous, this never happens to me."

She forces a smile and adds:

"It must be the beers plus the wine."

"Plus the spaghetti, plus the métro."

Come on, girl, say it, go ahead.

"Plus Paris, plus you."

Could something I no longer believed in really happen? It's hard to say. You need grace in these situations, and I've got these clumsy paws fumbling idiotic gestures.

This is the moment when the soup gets cold . . . and the first time I practically blow my nose on a tie. First time for a lot of things. At forty you can't exactly run up the banners. Panic is mounting.

"Listen," Philippe says, "I . . . well, I've known women and all, but I'm not exactly your super-technician. I . . ."

That's reassuring. *The Sensual Disaster,* starring Philippe Lipinchky and Jacqueline Puisset: a G-rated film, absolutely anti-erotic, recommended for children and students of religious schools.

On a bed. With a man. Me, a bookseller.

"Don't turn on the light."

"I won't."

They laugh. It's true he has naturally curly hair. Tonight I'm Rita Hayworth and I won't let this chance go by. I won't miss it, I can't. It's the only

one, this love, if it is one—the first and the last in
the aroma of velouté à la Marie-Thérèse or Marie-
Louise, don't know which and I don't care. . . .
Arsène is probably still talking out there. My God,
if Noëlle saw me now.

I can barely make out the geraniums in the shadows. My God, they're ugly, your geraniums, my
poor love, as ugly as we are, right now, the most
beautiful . . .

The wrestler's head rolls over on the pillow. Don't
leave, please don't leave. If you go, all my strength
will be gone.

On the other side of the pane the moon climbs out
of the night . . . a bitter sweetness and, finally, the
sea between the cliffs, a sudden unknown sea, the
sun nailed to the heart of a bed in the sky.

I reread: *Convention unexpectedly prolonged.*
Home Tuesday. All is well. Kisses. Jacqueline.

"Thank you," she whispers.

She carefully hangs up the phone, pulls up the
sheet, and turns with a sigh toward Philippe. He
just dropped off to sleep. Eight o'clock in the morning. Noëlle's bound to catch on. I don't give a damn.

God, it's one thing to savor love stories in books
and quite another to live one.

She shuts her eyes and curls up. Beyond the edge
of the window the city awakens. Hugging her knees,
Jacqueline falls asleep, rolled around a bubble of
happiness—a fragile, brilliant, comfortable balloon
to hold forever, an iridescent bubble, evasive for so
long.

It's broad daylight. Bedtime.

J'adore Mephisto King.

chapter twenty

THE arm falls on the mat, raising a cloud of dust in his nostrils.

"One!"

Philippe puts his weight on his heels, lifts his lower body, and attempts a bridge, which his adversary quickly crushes.

"Two!"

Philippe's right foot sweeps the mat and he deftly jackknifes to a standing position in the middle of the ring. He knocks his adversary off balance with a hair yank. The victim falls, wailing in pain, provoking an outcry of indignation from the crowd.

"Kill Mephisto!"

Philippe accentuates his contemptuous posture, casting a look of pure disdain on the packed bleachers. The tepid air smells of tobacco and canned beer.

Léon flies across the rectangle like a catapulted dragonfly. It's a four-person match: over there at the other end of the ring another adversary prances about outside the ropes. Weighing a hundred pounds less than Léon does, this one's a specialist in the donkey kick and facial friction, and is named Mauricette Duporinet, mother of four children, highly qualified professional wrestler.

A week ago they decided to accept mixed combat: men against women. Of course, they play the mean guys and get massacred by the two vengeful Amazons. The ladies keep their word too, that's for sure.

As a pro Philippe appreciates the way the blonde works: she varies her holds, has a good chop. The other one's good too, nice and supple. Real professionals. They chatted a little in the back before coming out. Mme. Duporinet's originally from the Drôme, married to a civil servant, and has problems communicating with her eldest son.

"The younger ones don't know about my profession—if they did they'd probably be scared to show me their report cards!"

They're both really nice, a tiny bit affected, maybe, when you first meet them. You can tell Léon has a weakness for the blonde, Fernande, who at this moment is trying with great enthusiasm to disconnect his shoulder blade. The audience is encouraging.

"Do it, Fernande, crush him!"

This match is ridiculous, but it was the manager's idea to attract more Saturday night fans. Will the pure young girls triumph over the Neanderthal man and the Infernal creature? It looks that way.

Léon crawls on all fours, dragging Fernande behind him amidst violent booing. Mephisto King leans over, tags his buddy, and jumps into the ring. Three minutes to go.

"Wanna have a drink afterwards?" Léon pants.

Philippe nods and nonchalantly lands a cross-ankle pickup. The lady soars through the air, he takes her off-balance, and shaking the ring with a synchronized thump of his heel, seems to break her in two over his knee.

Fernande rolls on the mat, imploring heaven, simulating the effects of a spinal column broken in seventy-two pieces. Mephisto wipes his hands calmly, but when the referee turns his back, he punches the air an eighth of an inch from Fernande's cheek. She takes the blow, falling back like an empty sack.

"Kill him! Can the referee!"

Mauricette is bouncing up and down, anxious to get in there.

I'll send a postcard, won't have time for a letter if we take the eleven seventeen express. I might as well tell her who we're wrestling against—have to make a living somehow!

Okay, it's all yours, sweet one!

Mauricette attacks as though her youngest had just broken a teacup from her Limoges set. Philippe staggers under the chop, gathers strength to help her get her hold, and collapses, groggy in the pincers. The audience is on its feet, screaming for vengeance.

Six inches from Philippe's eye, a furious, fat, ruddy-faced guy in the front row belches out:

"Bite him!"

Cro-Magnon shoots out, defying the rules, but Fernande, who has switched with Mauricette, thuds the hairy chest with parallel feet. Léon capsizes like the *Titanic,* lamentably collapsing on his pal with a foghorn bellow as the two women triumph in their vengeance against the criminals.

The two heavyweights stand up amid the booing and with enormous difficulty head for the dressing rooms.

I am no longer alone.

Of course we don't see each other too often, with our respective jobs, and Paris–Perpignan: we couldn't have done much better as far as distance goes. I've never taken the train so much in my life, and she comes as much as possible. We had a three-day escape to Toulouse—for me, an imaginary match, for her, an imaginary convention.

Next Sunday we decide what to do about this affair. Either we choose total illegality with episodic hotel rooms, clandestine letters, secret rendezvous, et cetera, or else, well, I don't know. . . .

"Hand me the towel, will ya?"

The soap bubbles slide across the arcades of Léon's prominent shoulders.

"Move it, man, can't keep the ladies waiting."

Philippe stretches out under the shower and rubs himself vigorously.

"What's got into you, Léon? You got ants in your pants or somethin'?"

The wrestler has trouble tying the knit tie around his bull's neck. Always the dandy. Cro-Magnon. Ever since I've known him. Usually, in this business it's more the sporty look—turtleneck and jacket. Never for him. We talked about it once. "Up to the age of seventeen I wore nothing but my old man's work clothes, so I've been making up for lost time ever since."

"Hurry up, Toto, one drink with the gals and we're off to the station."

Philippe dresses quickly, stashes his shoes, mask, tights, and cape in his overnight bag, and the two men walk out side by side.

The gymnasium is empty now. In the yellow vertical spotlight beams, workmen take down the stands. The ground is littered with candy wrappers and popsicle sticks.

"So how's your love life, still going strong?"

I didn't tell him much, but he understood. He's intuitive, Léon, you don't have to spell it out for him.

"It's going well. The only problem is that we live so far apart, we don't see each other too often."

The slap on the back resonates in the silence of the hallway.

"Ought to get married, my boy. Believe me, it's perfect for guys like us. Look at me—swell kids, the little woman, I'm all set. The good life."

Philippe sighs. It's true in a way, but nothing's that easy.

The two men are outside now, surrounded by tall buildings, gray moonlit teeth in the somber jaw of the city. It's completely deserted, not far from midnight. Everything seems mineral. At the corner, a solitary glow in the pale night: the Fantasia sign, brilliant mauve neon.

"Good thing the Viking's not here. We'd get ten years' worth of stories about him wrestling with chicks."

Philippe smiles.

"Léon, you got a strange definition of a chick."

Léon shrugs his bank-safe shoulders.

"What d'you expect in this business? You can't exactly be shaped like a starlet."

They push open the door. It's a classic bar like millions of others at the corners of shopping centers. Jukebox full blast. Mauricette and Fernande are at a table waiting for them.

Fernande Bollaert is slightly sausagelike in her imitation Chanel jacket. She sips her panaché, little finger in the air:

"You add twelve stitches per inch on the sides, continue straight with your jersey, take up at each end for the raglan, and don't forget to take in the collar. You should be able to get by with twelve balls, especially if you use size eight-and-a-half needles."

Mauricette listens to her partner's explanation, forehead wrinkled in concentration. She turns toward the two men.

"Another sweater—my kids wear things out so quickly," she says, "and what drives me crazy is that they just don't pay attention. I find all their things thrown all over the place."

Cro-Magnon laughs.

"You must spoil them."

"No, that's not it, it's the same with their studies. I have to keep a sharp eye on their notebooks, because otherwise it's the TV from morning to night. And my husband just isn't firm enough—he always gives in."

Philippe takes a sip of his drink. A wife with one hundred sixty-five pounds of muscle; he's probably right not to be too tough.

"It was a good match," Léon says. "You two do all right, I must say."

"It's true," Philippe adds. "My congratulations."

Their cheeks redden.

"We've done quite a few tours," Fernande admits. "We're a team. In Belgium we're quite a hit."

They laugh. They're nice people. Philippe wonders what brings two housewives in their thirties, motherly knitting types, to do leg dives and half nelsons for the Saturday night crazies.

"I was a typist," Mauricette says, "but I was zero for speed, my fingertips were too fat. So I recycled myself. . . . I can't complain."

"And me, I was a waitress," says Fernande. "One day a guy clobbered the boss and knocked out the waiter. I was the only personnel left. I had to intervene, he was breaking up everything, so I threw him out. After that, someone introduced me to a guy who had a place and was looking for girls to start up a number. It paid better than lemonade and was a lot less boring. That's how it started."

"It doesn't prevent a family life," remarks Mauricette. "I'm at home more now than when I worked at the office."

"And your husbands," Léon asks, "how do they take it?"

With an infinitely feminine, dignified air, Fernande brushes back her hair and lifts her panaché. She stifles a discreet burp and answers:

"Easy. Nice and easy."

At the other end of the bar a few locals are glued to the pinball machine.

Mustn't forget to send Jacqueline a postcard.

*   *   *

Léon keeps quiet. He takes his glass delicately, sips his drink, and puts it down.

Just don't pay any attention. This happens sometimes. It must be some form of mental illness—the excitement of danger. The problem is not that there are four of them, but that they've been drinking. Not enough to be really drunk, just enough to keep up the provocation.

The closest one lifts his beer, foam overflowing, and glides it along the bar, spraying the back of Philippe's hand. Philippe wipes it off discreetly and turns toward the two ladies.

"We've gotta go now, it's a good ten minutes from here to the station."

A short, stocky guy with a nose like a cliff leans over and poses his elbow and chin on the table.

"Do you have a moment, or is it that you don't like us? We're really nice, huh, Lucien, aren't we nice?"

Lucien, who's been trying desperately since he was fifteen to look like John Wayne, smooths back his Brylcreemed locks.

"In fact, we're damned nice, because if we weren't nice, you know what that'd be like, if we weren't nice?"

That one's the most dangerous. There's something abnormal in his eyes, a touch of the crazed snake. He probably hits before he knows why.

I never have understood this wild desire to get clobbered. If Léon and I get up, we'll make minced meat of them, they must know that. Maybe they also know we won't do it. There are always a few idiots hanging around after the match, looking for a fight. Why? A need for violence, a desire to affirm themselves, maybe, to parade around . . .

"Maybe you'd like to buy us a round. You must do okay, playing the clowns up there."

Léon is a real spectacle at moments like these— the serenity of the universe collected in a single man, the Andes on a spring morning. The ladies haven't budged. He looks at his watch and smiles at them.

"Let's go," he says.

"Hey, they're chicken, these guys, real yellow-bellies!"

I hadn't noticed that one before. He was clutching the pinball machine like a leech. Your basic gorgeous young kid. The girls must faint in his path and he knows it; in fact that's probably about all he knows.

Philippe raises his hand.

"Waiter, please."

The gorgeous kid looks at him and cracks a smile.

"What's wrong, fat man? You're all pale. You scared or somethin'?"

Think about something else . . . the watercolors, hmm, I haven't painted since Jacqueline came. She didn't exactly hide her feelings—she thought they were all hideous. Tough girl.

"Give 'em another round—gorillas have to drink, you know."

First crack in the Andes. A shiver in the flank of the mountain. Watch out for an avalanche.

The stocky kid's hand grazes Cro-Magnon's skull.

"You dust it every morning?"

Léon's a golden soul, really a good guy. And he's

doing them a favor. He could strangle all four of them with one hand. Léon's a true friend.

"Waiter, another round for the ladies and gentlemen."

The tattered bill lands on the table, followed instantly by its reflection upside down on the Formica.

The lady wrestlers are the first ones up.

John Wayne puts his hand on Lipinchky's chest.

"Pal, when I treat, you drink."

A ten-ton per cubic centimeter silence falls on the bar. These four worms have seen too many westerns on TV. I know these neighborhoods—it'll be years before the cops get here.

Philippe says nothing, just walks forward.

"You didn't get what I said, potato face?"

Philippe is amazed to see the punk fly into the air and land on the zinc counter amidst cocktails and cash register.

I had no idea I hit him so hard. A good slap, but no weight behind it. It was the potato face that did it. I can't control it, comes too close to home.

In a flash Philippe sees the owner pick up the telephone.

"Behind you."

Léon turns around and grabs the stocky kid by the shirt as he charges head first. Three tables collapse. With a flip of the hip Léon sends his assailant across the bar without touching the ground. Fernande flings her bag into the gorgeous kid's face; he backs up punching.

Mauricette screams. Philippe dives to protect her. John Wayne backs up, bottle in hand.

The owner disappears under the bar, comes back with a bludgeon.

This is a real Western, Philippe thinks, but it's time to stop fooling around . . .

The bottle explodes level with his head.

"Stop!" the owner shouts.

His voice cracks. A knife shines in a nervous hand.

"Careful," Mauricette says.

Cro-Magnon takes a chair and flings it at the kid with the knife, but he dodges it.

"Get out quick, I'll hold him."

"Not fast enough, Léon. If you get stuck, I'll never forgive myself."

"Over here, sonny."

The guy pivots. There's terror in his eyes. If he wasn't afraid, he'd be long gone by now—the panicky ones are always the worst.

In a flash of neon the blade skims the jacket. Philippe grabs an arm, twists, and lands a powerful punch. Léon sighs with relief as he looks up to see a police car stop in front of the bar, lights off.

Philippe sucks his bleeding fingers, a big smile across his face.

"We're happy to see you. We were starting to get desperate."

"Put your hands over your heads."

"But . . ."

Léon's the first to obey. It's true the decor does not exactly plead in our favor—four guys spread on the floor, one with a nose bigger than his head and blood dripping down his lap.

"Listen, officer . . ."

"Okay, you'll have your chance to explain later. Let's get going, all of you out of here."

The night slaps them in the face. The policemen

telephone. There's not a single button left on my shirt.

"We're gonna miss our train," Léon murmurs.

Next to the officers, Fernande and Mauricette confer breathlessly. The four troublemakers have a hard time gathering themselves together.

In the dark car a square jawbone is vaguely lit by the dashboard lights.

"You're wrestlers—that's not going to help your story much, you know."

Philippe grits his teeth. This could get us thrown out of the league. This whole circus for those four lousy jerks . . . it's too good to be true.

"Come on, get in."

Only thing missing's the sirens, like in American movies.

The tough guy with the rapier is holding his head in both hands, and he could probably use a third.

"You're the one who hit that guy?"

There's a nuance of admiration in his voice.

"He was armed. I didn't have time to fool around."

The motor starts up.

She's gonna find out—I can tell she's gonna find out. I have no idea how it'll happen, but with my luck, it couldn't go any other way.

That'll teach me to go to those places. It's all I need—carted off to the pokey for fighting. She's no prude, but it's not gonna make her happy, that's for sure.

Plus, God knows how it'll be presented. Already, my physique goes against me. It's true I've got the mug of quite a brute. I'm surprised they didn't handcuff me. She's gonna find out. No question, I'm gonna have problems with this one.

So this is what it's like to have a sweetheart, my good man. Before, something like this just glided right past me; now, I'm afraid of getting scolded. Or worse, it might disgust her or shock her. Of course, with her books, she's not likely to get carted off by cops. Who knows, she might even want to break it off; no, probably not. It's Léon's fault, all this; he's the one who set up this crazy scheme. I never should have gone along with it. Wrestling with women . . . why not with newborn babies?

God, this van stinks. What a lovely evening!

The gray night passes by the iron-grated windows, cut by concrete and streetlamps.

chapter twenty-one

"NOTHING new?"

Morani takes a drag off his Gitane, pushes up his glasses, and scratches his nose. He asks out of habit, knowing full well no one will ever answer him.

I hate this job. Everything, right up to the noise of the teletapes, exasperates me. At night in the editing room it's enough to kill you.

Morani, the man renowned for whipping off six columns in three minutes. Sure, he used to do that . . .

Jealous of her son, she delivers him to the police. . . . Empty, no fantasy, not even any blood.

The most successful story in fifteen years was the one about the cat who covered one hundred miles to find its owners. That was ideal, especially since he took the highway. Too bad it doesn't happen every week. It's perfect for the headlines.

Telephone. I'm surprised it hasn't rung before;

it's been fifteen seconds now I've had my ass on this chair.

"Hello, yeah, this is Morani."

". . ."

"Hi, you got somethin' for me?"

It'll be the first time in his life if he does, but when you're desperate, you have to fantasize a little bit.

"Where are you?"

Where else could he be? Playing cards in the dungeon of the police station waiting for glory to cross his path. He's what you call our special correspondent from the provinces. He probably had ambition at some point too.

When I took this rag, we had 325,000 readers. I fought for thirty years, received and made millions of phone calls, typed billions of letters, blew my stack five thousand times, smoked six truckloads of tobacco, and today we're at 170,000. If you call that a success, you can consider yourself an optimist. We've run everything: movie stars' loves, secret unclaimed children—fantastic, that one: Tino Rossi's unclaimed child, Fernandel's unclaimed child, Hallyday's, Poniatowski's. . . . After that it was first loves. Antoinette Dudevent, farmer's wife in the Loiret, was the first love of . . . who shall it be this week? Einstein? Léon Blum? Johnny Weissmuller? Al Capone? With three pictures and plenty of spaces you can crank it out in fifteen minutes.

"Okay, go ahead, I'm listening."

In fact, I'm not listening, I'm daydreaming. I'm thirsty and sleepy and there's no bed and no beer.

The cigarette goes out. Morani loosens his tie.

"What did you say his pseudonym was? . . .
Mephisto King, yeah, has a certain ring to it. No
problem for the photos, we've got 'em in the sports
archives. And the other one?"
Cro-Magnon. Quite a pair—Hell and the pre-
historic. Maybe I'll even sharpen my pencil.
"What d'you say they did, these two cuties?"
Barroom brawl. Couple of broken tables, not
even a real injury.
"How many were they up against? . . . "Four?
Well, let's say twelve and leave it at that."
Morani's torso leans over the ashtray.
"What d'you say? Say that again . . ."
" . . . "
"Two lady wrestlers? So they were protecting
them?"
" . . . "
"The girls don't have pseudonyms? No? Doesn't
matter, we'll find some. That all you got on it?"
Morani spits into the trashcan under his desk,
hangs up the phone, picks it up again, yawns, and
decides:
"We're redoing number one. Send a guy to docu-
mentation. Two wrestlers: Lipinchky, called Mephisto King; Léon Duvert, called Cro-Magnon. And
two pictures of lady wrestlers. Doesn't matter which,
a blonde and a brunette, and send it to the lab for
touch-ups. We need 'em big and tough, but still a
bit of the pinup type. And move it."
Headline first, the essential:

FOR THE LOVE OF WANDA THE TIGRESS AND
FAIR-HAIRED TANYA, THE KING OF HELL AND

CRO-MAGNON MAN DEVASTATE THE SLEEPING
CITY.

The keys patter away—this is the kind of thing
that flows by itself. I can do it and think about something else at the same time.

> We've seen them in the ring. Unpardoning
> blows—colossals with no rules and no pity,
> who no longer dare fight with their faces
> exposed.

I won't take home the Pulitzer with that, but I've
done worse. Four characters, violence, passion; the
whole salad's there—nothing left to do but add the
dressing and toss.

> Hunted down and despised, the two men
> delve deeper and deeper into bestiality with
> every match. But one particularly savage night,
> as the cries from the crowd excited their ani-
> mal instincts, the spark of passion that never
> expires completely, even in the hardest soul,
> blazed into a fire that ravaged the two abomi-
> nable fighters: Two women appeared, long
> hair flowing, biceps flexed, bloodthirsty jaws,
> Wanda the brunette and Tanya the blonde.
> Love flamed quickly under the thick skulls.

After all, it'll be great publicity for them. This
kind of article could triple their intake. I should
even get in touch with them, set up some kind of
deal.

Morani spits out a mixture of paper, tobacco, and saliva, turns his cigarette around, and laboriously lights the sizzling, wet end.

They could go on tour . . . "The Furious Lovers" or something like that, a sex and violence spectacle. First I love you, then I clobber you . . .

Morani flips over in his armchair.

We'll rent a circus tent, a caravan, a publicity campaign—it'll be a gold rush with a story like that. We could even take it to the United States. "Wrestler's Love," I can see it now at Madison Square Garden.

> . . . and that night, like every night, in the obscure streets of the outskirts of town, where delinquents breed like rabbits, the neon sign was flashing outside the neighborhood bar. It's here that Mephisto and Wanda, Tanya and Cro-Magnon, come after their murderous combat, to hide their torrential love. But that night the gang was out. Hunched over their Yamahas, passing around their hashish cigarettes, they're easy to recognize. A dozen or so who for months have spread terror in the land, racing through quiet streets, drunk with speed, living off looting, the studs of their black leather jackets shining in the moonlight . . .

The door opens; Cornillon shoves his belly against Morani's desk and throws two pictures into the chaos of papers and ashtrays.

"Here you go—nothing special to add really. Lipinchky was born in '40 in Courbevoie; Duvert two years before in Hénin-Liétard, used to be a miner."

Morani takes a drag and nods.

"Okay, take that to composition with a caption for each. For Duvert, something like, 'Just as his ancestors took refuge in caves, every day he would descend into the belly of the earth.' For Lipinchky, something along the lines of 'Obsessed with Hell, he chose to be the devil of the ring.' Okay, get going."

Cornillon salutes, opens the door, and turns around, scratching his belly.

"One of the lady wrestlers has four kids. Could we do something with that?"

Morani coughs, crushes his cigarette butt, and attacks his machine.

"See what you can come up with. Try something like, 'As her children cried in the stairway, she quivered in the arms of the colossus.' You got ten minutes to get that going. I'll be right down with the paper."

He types four sentences, lights another cigarette. A quick conclusion and it's in the bag. A job well done, sure to thrill the subscribers.

Okay, let's go, gotta get this finished.

A pale, early light invaded the construction sites as the dazed lovers found themselves handcuffed and, with the dawn, crept into the police station. Behind them, their victims stirred feebly, consciousness barely filtering through their brains fogged with alcohol and punches. But together they staggered in, surrounded by officers. Again we see, even for such disgraced beings, the tremendous miracle of love still alive.

chapter twenty-two

"AND did ya see when he made a tornado with his head right when she jumped on him and tried to flatten him?"

"Yes, I saw that too, it was splendid."

"She's a good wrestler, that lady, huh, Tata? She's hefty too, huh?"

"Very good, dear, and she's very hefty in fact. Muscles everywhere—a little cellulite, too, here and there."

"Still, he shoulda won, 'cause he's a lot stronger, you can tell, huh, can't you?"

Jacqueline glances at her watch.

"Yes, you can tell . . . okay, uh, I've got to go because . . ."

"You know when he's gonna be on TV again?"

"I don't know, dear, but I wouldn't miss it for anything. So, uh . . ."

"And did ya see when he went in with Cro-Magnon to sandwich the blonde?"

"Yes, I saw that too. I've got to hang up because I . . ."

"What does that mean, Tata, the 'Furious Lovers'?"

"Furious. That means . . . uh, listen, you ask your mother because I'm in a bit of a hurry right now and . . ."

"You sellin' books?"

"Yes, that's it, you see, I try to sell books, like a lot of booksellers I know. So, a big hug and a kiss, thanks for calling . . ."

"And did ya see how he got out of the bear hug?"

Jacqueline gently massages her forehead, where a migraine has insidiously placed its first thorn.

". . . with a double nelson," she sighs.

"Yeah, and a kick to top if off. It was a swell match."

"Really swell. See you later, André."

She hangs up. A deep breath and it rings again. She lets out the breath.

"Oh, it's you. I was just going to call you."

Receiver under her chin, she thumbs through two notebooks at a time and grabs a pencil with her free hand. Only my feet are left unoccupied—I could try typing with my toes . . .

"Okay, listen, I need a whole assortment of paperbacks, so I'll send you the numbers. Plus I need six copies of *I'm Expecting a Baby,* by Laurence Pernoud."

For all the time she's been expecting that baby, she must be surprised it hasn't come yet.

"That's all. Thank you."

Jacqueline hangs up and turns around, ferocious,

toward Fabienne. For forty-five minutes she's been attempting the delicate accord between eyeshadow and eyeliner in the corner of her right eye.

"You wouldn't mind taking care of the new arrivals, would you?"

Startled, Fabienne heads back toward the cardboard boxes.

I am about to explode.

When I say I'm about to explode, I am underestimating the situation. And that stupid idiot Noëlle still hasn't gotten here. Sure, when you don't need people they're always there, but as soon as . . . okay, don't get too excited, or you'll burst into a million pieces.

That'd be a nice headline for their pigsty of a newspaper: "Fiery bookseller explodes in her own store; pieces dispersed on best-seller rack."

Almost as spectacular as "The king of Hell and Cro-Magnon man devastate the sleeping city for the love of what d'ya call it-the-Beautiful and who knows which Queen of the Jungle . . ."

As Noëlle says, "You're certainly not going to believe everything they put in that kind of rag, are you?"

Of course not, but still, it's true that ever since then the four of them have been wrestling together.

A wild success, it seems, all over France: "The Muscled Lovers, 850 pounds of violence and passion gone wild," so the posters say. I even had the privilege of seeing it last night, and in color. Channel One.

And where do I come in, in the midst of those eight hundred fifty pounds, with my hundred and ten?

He's great, this nice peaceful man with his watercolors, his Mary Tudor lambchops, and his visits to
mother every Sunday.

He really filled my head with his stories. Sure, I
know they exaggerate, but still, there definitely was
a fight, and anyway, where there's smoke, there's
fire . . .

"Excuse me, I'd like a book on the upkeep of
plants for the apartment, because, you see, I . . ."

"In the back on the right, bottom shelf on the
left."

God, I've got to stop snapping back like that. I'll
start shattering glass and terrorizing my customers.

Still not noon. Or else my watch has stopped.
What could she be doing? This time she can't tell
me their clock is slow or that the little one is
teething . . .

What are they up to, those kids hovering around
the cookbooks? Always the same—it takes twelve
of them to buy one fifty-centime ball-point pen.

"Fabienne!"

Strange, for a while now she's been developing
this habit of leaping into the air and pedaling emptiness when all I do is call her, very politely.

"*Hhhhyes,* Mademoiselle?"

Hhhhyes, Mademoiselle, I'll *hhh*yes mademoiselle you, young lady.

"We're closing, you can go. I'll clean up myself."

I'd just as soon have no one in the store when my
dear little sister arrives.

And to top if off I've sold nothing this week. It's
as though suddenly all those jerks decided to stop
reading, assuming they ever knew how. Even Trotsky's let me down. I've had his *Gondolas of Desire*

and *Seguidillas for Dolores* under the counter for
a week now, and Monsieur can't be bothered to
come pick up his nonsense. Now everyone's gone
but Fabienne and me.

Trotsky.

He's out of breath, the poor man. He must have
run here from the square.

He stops. Fabienne is nearby with a pile of Jules
Vernes in her arms. He smiles vaguely and walks
toward me.

"You're closing, Mademoiselle Puisset. I'm afraid
I'm bothering you."

I dig up a smile . . . it's about time.

Just in time for the machine-gun round.

But it wasn't a machine-gun round. It was the
Jules Vernes cascading to the floor.

Stupefied, I look at Fabienne. Trotsky turns
around as well.

It's not the fact that she dropped the books that
gets me, it's her face.

Livid. Wild with rage and desperation. Reproach
incarnated. We're about to be treated to a nervous
breakdown. I walk around the cash register to go
toward her so at least she won't collapse. But what
happened?

"Fabienne, what . . ."

"Oh you, leave me alone."

Her voice pierces my brain. Suddenly I'm a little
bit afraid. This beautiful, sweet girl who never talks
suddenly . . .

She heads for Trotsky who instinctively moves
back.

Incredible, it's the *Walkyrie* and she's Brünhilde.

"Am I transparent, Monsieur Javier?"

His mouth opens and shuts twice before he finds
a tiny thread of a voice, which stammers:

"B-b-but, not at all, Mademoiselle, not at all."

"Then if I'm not transparent, why do you go to
the back of the store to ask for information when
I'm standing right in front of you?"

"But, but, but . . ." Trotsky says.

He stops there and seems to think that'll do as an
explanation, but Fabienne doesn't seem to agree.

"I'm too stupid, right? That's what you're trying
to tell me, isn't it?"

"Fabienne!"

Taking no notice whatsoever of my outburst, she
is practically screaming:

"I'm the potted plant, I am, you just walk right
past. I couldn't possibly understand your poems."

Her voice cracks and on come the tears. The peak
crisis past, a trembling starts up. When I walk toward her, she flails her arms, turns the paperback
book stand over on me, and collapses in my arms.
And this joker looks like he's going to collapse too.

"Well, do something, for goodness' sake!"

"Well, yes, I, uh, of course, certainly, naturally,
uh, but what?"

It's terrible: she's trembling so much she's shaking me. My shirt is soaked.

"Now, now, Fabienne."

What can I tell her? How can I console her? I
don't even know what this is all about!

"I'll get you something to drink."

"No."

She frees herself, runs down the aisle and out
into the sun. She's gone. I hope she doesn't do anything stupid.

I turn around. This imbecile is still planted there, breathless.

"What are you standing there for? Run after her, damn it!"

"You really think I . . ."

I'm shaking with rage. Finally he gets going in starts and stops, then hop! . . . he's gone.

It's true I just don't have enough problems right now; everything's going so well, it's nothing if my salesgirl blows up and attacks the clientele. Calm down, Jacqueline, take it easy. And my sister, what has become of her?

There she is. No kidding around with greetings or formalities; Noëlle is in full swing.

"I'm not too late, am I? You've already closed? Your blouse is wet . . . you look great, though. Have you been waiting long? François's got the flu again. He went out without a coat again, so what do you expect?"

A tornado. This woman is a tornado. She makes me dizzy.

"Noëlle, I have something important to tell you."

She stops. I must have a sober look on my face to cut her off like that. She has a sly look on her face.

"I bet you heard from Philippe."

"I have not heard from Philippe. Philippe is on tour with six hundred pounds of violence and passion and certainly doesn't have time to uncap a pen. No, what I wanted to ask you . . ."

There you have it: I'm dying for her to get here, and now here she is and I'm a wreck. I have all the symptoms of complete panic: burning ears, sweaty palms, stomach cramps. Come on, it's the only solution.

"Okay, here it is. It's not too complicated and won't surprise you a bit. In fact, all you have to do is cross the street."

Mouth open wide, Noëlle contemplates her sister. God, she looks stupid like that.

She might be more beautiful than I am, but with that expression she looks as thick as they come. Even at an early age she was like that—you had to explain things for hours before there'd be a tiny glimmer on the dim horizon of comprehension.

"Explain yourself," Noëlle says. "Why do I have to cross the street?"

What did I tell you? Noëlle Louberan, née Puisset, the most amazing example of feminine intuition to be found in all Languedoc-Roussillon. I'll have to spell it out, since dropping hints doesn't seem to do the trick.

"Noëlle, what is on the other side of the street?"

My voice is pure sweetness and light: millions of soft little flowers dance between each syllable.

"A bakery."

She thinks it over and continues:

"You want me to get you some croissants—you haven't had breakfast, right?"

"That's it, I called you last night to ask you to come across town to go buy me some croissants from the bakery right across the street. Bravo. You're getting more intelligent every day."

Noëlle Louberan jumps up in protest.

"Well, if you won't explain yourself, I have to invent something!"

"You're inventing nonsense."

"Don't scream!" Noëlle shouts. "If you scream, I'm leaving."

"I'm not screaming!" Jacqueline bellows. "But make an effort, damn it!"

Noëlle camps herself in front of the window and recites:

"On the other side of the street there is a bakery —that's not it. Next door there's a five-and-ten, next to the five-and-ten there's a door; next to the door there's another door, then two windows; after the two windows there's the pharmacy and . . ."

"Stop."

Noëlle stops. Jacqueline goes behind the counter and sits down.

"That's it. You hit it after all. You're going to the pharmacy."

"To do what?"

I'll have steam coming out of my nostrils if she keeps this up.

"To say hello to the pharmacist, what do you think? Listen, Noëlle, are you doing this on purpose or what?"

"I swear I'm not."

"Then that's even worse. Listen to me: You're going to go into the pharmacy and you're going to ask for . . ."

There it goes—complete block in the vocal cords.

Jacqueline makes a supreme effort, whistles the first four notes of the *Internationale,* and forces out:

"You ask for a test."

"What test?"

Atrocious crime in Perpignan bookstore: Bookseller suffocates her battered sister, forcing her to swallow a twelve-volume encyclopedia.

Jacqueline Puisset makes sure the door is locked, that nothing around them might fly away, takes a deep breath, throwing her torso out to gather strength, and thunders:

"The test to see if you're pregnant!"

The echo rolls slowly through the bookstore. Little by little it calms down. Like the soft clouds that come after a storm has been chased away by silence, tranquility returns . . . .

Noëlle opens one eye, verifies that the ceiling hasn't fallen in, that there're no cracks in the walls, and in her little-girl-on-prize-day voice sings out:

"Oh, because you . . ."

"Obviously we. . . . Anyway, it's partially your fault, all this time telling me it isn't healthy—what do you expect? Eventually it got to me."

Stunned, Noëlle protests in a weepy whine:

"But you can't say it's my fault if you . . ."

Crack. It was a good dam, but nothing compared to the strength of sisterly tears. If I cry, she cries—it's as straight a bet as the lines in this accounting notebook. That reminds me, I have to order three dozen tomorrow for the industrial college.

"My God, my God, but you're not sure, are you?"

"Don't whine like that, it's me it's happening to, not you. Of course I'm not sure; if I were sure I wouldn't be asking you to buy me a test."

Undone, Mother Noëlle looks at me as though I'm going to give birth in fifteen seconds.

"Why haven't you already checked with . . ."

"Listen to me. If I go into the pharmacy and ask Monsieur Papinelli for a test, in the space of half an hour the scandal will have exploded across town: Mademoiselle Puisset at the bookstore is pregnant by God knows who. I'll lose three-fourths of my customers; the oldies around the cathedral will shoot

me down with their stares! I'll be feeding the grape-
vine for years. So please, just do what I ask . . ."

Noëlle stands up like Bonaparte on the Pont
d'Arcole and utters her proclamation:

"Here I go. I'll be right back," she says.

Jacqueline watches her through the window as
she goes into the pharmacy. It won't be positive. It's
fatigue, nerves. At forty it's really not likely. . . .
Now at least I'll know . . . in fact, I already know,
it's just to confirm it. The proof is that I bought
Pernoud's book. I ordered six so no one would
suspect anything, but anyway, I'm practically sure.
God, tonight I'm leading the ciné-club debate and
I don't even know what it's on.

Here she comes with her little package.

Jacqueline, dear, now you'll know if that little
Mephisto is there or not.

Noëlle glues the telephone against her ear and
whispers.

"So?"

"Yes."

"Ah!"

End of conversation. Noëlle sits down gently on
the floor and distractedly pulls handfuls of yarn
out of the carpet.

chapter twenty-three

HERE she comes.

Today she looks more like the romantic heroines of Trotsky's poetry than ever—red eyes and all.

"I'm so sorry for . . ."

I bring her in, arm around her shoulders. I like you. Fabienne, I envy you, but I like you. It must be fairly rare to be hideously jealous of someone you really like. Especially now that I know how unhappy you are, inexplicably unhappy. I'm almost ready to tell you about my insane predicament, my catastrophic love story . . . *le bébé*. A nice big baby to make you forget your woes. Frankenstein consoling Greta Garbo—even better, pregnant Frankenstein consoling Greta Garbo.

"Come on, why don't we make some coffee?"

I've still got the little stove in the back. The pile of boxes is trembling in her hands. She sniffs, blows her nose, and here we go again—the Fountain of

Trévise. Well, dear, no big problems these days, you can look after your salesgirl a bit.

"Try to tell me about it, Fabienne, nice and slow, take a deep breath."

She takes a deep, gurgling breath and lets out a sob that makes the walls tremble.

"I am so unhappy."

So she says.

Bravo. That's a great explanation. But to look at her, I'd almost believe it. Maybe I should ask if her boyfriend's a wrestler; that would explain a lot.

I'll be motherly, it's good practice.

"But how could you be unhappy? You're so pretty, you like your job, you . . ."

Another downpour, stronger than ever. That was not the thing to say. In the long staccato wailing, I vaguely detect a stupefying sentence:

"No one pays any attention to me."

No one pays any attention to her? That's completely ridiculous. This girl stands out like a beacon —a true marvel, the beauty of Perpignan, from Saint-Jacques to Saint-Martin, from Haut-Vernet to La Garrigole, she shines in all her . . .

Here it comes, spilling out all at once:

"It's always you they talk to—all the customers— I'm always left alone. If I walk up, they take one look at me and take off, as though they're afraid or something. You must have noticed it. It's as though I had scurvy."

Barely able to breathe, I finally mutter:

"But still, there are men who, it seems to me, are not totally insensible to . . ."

She jerks back in revolt.

"If you knew what they say to me, you'd see why

I choose not to continue the conversation. You
think it's normal that the only people who talk to
me are satyrs?"

I sit down slowly. This burst of sorrow is completely genuine. Fabienne, I've always envied you
so much, could beauty also be a kind of solitude?

"Take Monsieur Javier. As soon as he sees me
he races back to you to recite a poem. You think
people recite poems to me? I get pinched on the
rear, that's what I get . . ."

Poor Fabienne, she's absolutely crushed. I was
so locked into my ugliness I never understood that
beauty can be a prison too. What a picture we make!
I'm the one comforting you, I'm the one with the
better deal: poems read to me, babies made in me;
and you, trapped in the store, provoking either terror in the timid ones or passionate attacks from the
wolves.

Suddenly I'm talking to her as though she's family.

"But you have a boyfriend, don't you? Someone
who cares for you?"

She shakes her head, spraying me with droplets.

"It's not as easy as you think. The ones I like
never dare to . . ."

Inaccessible. That's the word I've been looking
for. Inaccessible perfection. They take one look at
her and give up. She discourages everyone. Probably
nine-tenths of the people around here think she's
way too good for them. Result: She's alone and I
have another soaked blouse.

"What we need," I tell her, "is a good shot of
whiskey. I think there's some upstairs."

A shadow of a smile passes over her face

and I run upstairs. I always have a bottle for the salesmen.

An image comes to me. It was a few hours ago: in the store, Fabienne and me. Trotsky arrives. Fabienne explodes, with her forgotten, useless beauty, a beauty that isolates like a barrier . . . me and my walleye . . . and him with his head spinning with quotations and meandering poems. He comes to see me, so he must be lonely too. Maybe intelligence and sensibility isolate as well. There we were, the three of us, together, oblivious to each other's loneliness.

I come down with the bottle. A good shot of this will give us some courage, and God knows we both need it. I stop, one leg floating in midair.

I can't: no alcohol in my condition!

A low blow. I'll have to look through Laurence Pernoud, but I think I remember Noëlle cutting out cocktails when she was pregnant. What a bore. Fabienne takes hers down in one gulp and shuts her swollen eyes.

I'm thinking. There's a question buzzing around in my head. I've got to ask her.

"Fabienne . . ."

"Yes."

"Have you ever been envious of me?"

She swallows, winces, looks at the floor.

"Many times."

It's almost time to open the store. I feel like a storm has wrung out my body. Perhaps I'll never be the same. Not because I'm carrying a child, but because a pretty-faced girl has been jealous of Mademoiselle Puisset, the ugly one, the walleyed one, the one nobody likes.

Fabienne makes an effort to finish her drink. I turn away because I don't want her to see that now I'm the one who's crying, even if these are the sweetest tears I've ever shed . . .

What did the weatherman say this morning? Oh, yes. Clear skies throughout the area.

Jacqueline laughs out loud at the sight of the Louberans' sunken expressions.

"It's ideal—couldn't have worked out better. Forty years old: it'll be an old people's baby, thus subject to all possible defects. Plus, what with the respective physiques of his mom and pop, he'll look more like Frankenstein than anyone else. Then I'll have to close the store and go to Switzerland to give birth, like the Queen of England. Then, either it's welfare or I bring him back under my arm, saying I found him one morning on the side of the highway, and no one will believe me, of course. That's the way the situation looks to me. What do you think? Say something."

François wrinkles his brow.

"I didn't know the Queen of England gave birth in Switzerland."

Noëlle shrugs her shoulders, takes a big gulp of aperitif, refills Jacqueline's glass, slams down the bottle, and cries out:

"Jacqueline, get married!"

Jacqueline lets out a dry, sarcastic laugh.

"To a masked wrestler, lover of Wanda the Bengal Tigress?!"

Noëlle looks sadly at her sister, coughs, and slides this out like a swan on a lake:

"But you, well, you don't dislike each other. You

say he's a wrestler, but what does that mean, a wrestler? It's as though I said of you, 'Oh, she's a bookseller.' He does play with the children."

François looks at his watch and shifts his feet.

"We're going to be late, it's starting right now."

"Of course, I could have an abortion. That would solve everything."

"You could at least see each other first of all. He doesn't wrestle all the time. You could at least talk to him about it."

Jacqueline reaches for the bottle, serves herself again, and contemplates her cohorts.

"Forty years old, married to a monster who gets slaughtered every night by the Bermuda Panther . . . behind a mask. Not to mention the fights in bars. And here I am, surrounded by the small-town bourgeoisie coming in to buy *The Guide to Perfect Savoir-Vivre* and *How to Behave in Society* . . ."

I go on and on, but I know I'm not fooling anyone, least of all myself—it's just a game. It's all for show. Of course I've got to tell him and, well, he is attached to me. We'll figure out something . . . some sort of solution. On top of it, I'm afraid. You just don't have a baby like that—nothing to it. A newborn baby, a . . . my God, I'm going to have one! Eveything was all worked out, right up to retirement, then pow! A kid running up and down the aisles.

François gets up.

"Listen, talking about it now is getting us nowhere. You're just going around in circles, and I must remind you we are already late."

I'll have to act completely normal, smile at everyone. "How are you, Mademoiselle Puisset?" "How is Mademoiselle Puisset? Well, she seems to be fine."

You'd better believe she's fine. She's in the process of creating a future expert in pile drivers and the half nelson.

Not to mention that if he takes after his father, he'll be a good thirty pounds at birth, and who gets the fun of bringing him into this world? Another little pleasure to look forward to. She gets all the honors, Mademoiselle Puisset does.

François puts the car into first and starts off gently, as though transporting a pregnant woman.

"We'll end up circling for an hour before we find a place. Would've been easier to walk."

He says that every time. My God, it was nice when everything was orderly. If I shut my eyes really tight, if I really want it, maybe I can go back in time and nothing would have happened, it'd just be an evening like any other. I'm a woman of the provinces; I love this soft weather, the sleepy winters. The snow in the mountains behind me is a barrier against external dangers; sadness cannot penetrate, the land protects me. I don't want to leave this place. If this baby comes, I want him to run down the promenade, to know summers in the shade of the palms and plane trees . . .

"There's a place right there."

François parks. Noëlle slips her arm under her sister's as they walk into the hall of the ciné-club. It's an unusual gesture for her. It's not that we don't love each other, it's just not a habit with us. When we were little, if we touched each other it was because we were fighting. I know what she's telling me

right now: that she's with me, that she's sad, happy,
ecstatic, panicky, thrilled, and that in any case, she's
there, and she'll always be there, and that's so good
for me to know. . . . A child. My own child.

chapter twenty-four

VICTORIA carefully places her portion of *tarte aux épinards* on her plate and sniffs suspiciously. Looking at it, one gets the distinct impression that the hors d'oeuvre has been through three shipwrecks, four earthquakes, and five or six fires. Smelling it, you'd say it's definitely burnt. Tasting it, you'd swear it was flaming sponge à la dishwater.

In a spirit of self-sacrifice Victoria Lipinchky chews, swallows with difficulty, and pushes away her plate.

"Something," she says, "is troubling you."

Making a special effort, Philippe raises an eyebrow and proclaims with absolutely no conviction:

"Not at all, why?"

The accusing finger of the ex-garment worker points at the disgrace resting on her plate.

"Your first unsuccessful *tarte* in over twenty years."

Philippe scratches his chin, completely distracted.

"It's not one of my best, but you have to admit that's a pretty weak indication."

Victoria's tiny fist bangs the table and bounces back.

"You call that 'not one of your best'? Well, that's your privilege, but I'd like to know what you were thinking about when you were making it, the Second World War?"

If I tell her she'll fly out of her chair and I'll have to explain everything from A to Z. It'd probably be good for me, of course, but as long as it's not settled, I'm keeping my mouth shut.

Victoria comes around the table and puts her hand on her son's shoulder.

When he's sitting down, he's a tiny bit shorter than she is.

"Tell me about it or I'll pull your big ears. Are you sick of losing? Is that it? You'd like to win from time to time?"

"No, that's not it."

"Then what is it?"

At this point she's not about to give up her prey. Down below, only an occasional car goes by this Sunday; it's raining and the Parisians stayed home. The asphalt of the exit ramps shines under the droplets. A sad landscape.

I've got a match at five o'clock at Choisy.

Victoria takes her son's ear between her delicate fingers.

"Watch out, I'm going to pull."

He didn't laugh; it must be worse than I thought.

"I've got it, it's Wanda the Lioness who's making you suffer. I saw right away she was bad news."

"Wanda the Tigress," Philippe says, "and she's

not making me suffer at all. She has four kids who
give her plenty to do."

The elderly lady crosses her arms.

"Well, when I think of that poster: 'The Furious
Lovers' . . . it creates a strange impression. People
must think . . ."

"All you have to do is listen to the audience for
two minutes and you'll know what they think."

"So what is it? What's wrong?"

Phillipe looks at his mother, scratches his chin,
and realizes he forgot to shave. Suddenly, like
throwing his adversary onto the mat, he lets loose:
"I'm in love."

Don't move, Victoria, no tears, no bursts of joy;
the earth will move back to its place. . . . Don't explode and don't collapse.

The old curse is finally fading: the young woman
leaning on the wall of the school watching the other
mothers no longer wants to kill them. Nothing is so
exhausting as being constantly jealous. Thirty years
later, this kid who makes people laugh finally ap-
peals to a woman.

Just like other people . . .

Dear God, whether you exist or not, in any case,
thank you. I, Victoria Lipinchky, have made a son
like other sons. I can't be too hard on myself, it
wasn't so bad, because now you see . . . I must have
been too difficult. A mother's eye, as they say.

Everything will change for you now, Philippe. If
only you knew how you need that change! Your
geraniums, your simmering *tartes,* your cheese mix-
tures—it was killing you, my dear boy. You can't
fill your life with watercolors and spinach. They
were killing me too, your little habits, your solitude.

It's true that for years I've been waiting expectantly every Sunday for the doorbell to ring, that it gives me a lot of pleasure to see you standing there with your basket and your smile, but from now on it's going to be something else. I'm going to ask you a lot of idiotic questions, but don't be angry; you must know your old mother's just too happy to be very intelligent.

And even if it doesn't last, at least you will have had that, it will have happened to you, for you.

"You've got nothing to say?"

Mme. Lipinchky quivers, begins a tiny leap into the air, checks it, and joins her hands, Virgin Mary style.

"Who is it? Is she a proper girl?"

"What do you mean, proper?"

Victoria pulls up her chair and gets comfortable.

"You never tell me anything. I have to drag everything out of you. What does she do?"

"She lives far away," Philippe says. "She's a bookseller, and she's not exactly young."

Victoria's eyes widen.

"A bookseller! That's wonderful, now that's a profession!"

"Not like mine, I know, I know."

The brightness in her eyes suddenly fades under the arch of her wrinkled brow.

"What exactly do you mean by 'she's not exactly young'?"

"Fortyish," Philippe says.

Eyes and mouth round out in stupefaction.

"Forty! You call that not exactly young? How old do you want her to be? You want her to be a teen-ager?"

"I never said that."

"And why didn't you tell me about her before?"

"Well, because . . ."

"Have you made plans? Do you think you'll . . ."

Philippe sniffs, jumps up, catches his falling chair, runs into the kitchen, and opens the oven: the roast beef looks like post-Nero Rome.

His mother has followed him into the kitchen, eyes glued on her son. She sits down on the stool she uses for peeling vegetables.

I've prayed so much, my big, muscular baby with your misshapen face, and it's finally happened. A woman has come, and I've waited for her for so long—even more than for the Messiah—and she's finally come. A bookseller! Think of how much this woman must have read. I . . .

"But you've got to get married, then."

Philippe looks at his mother, pops a cherry into his mouth, spits out the seed, and says:

"Well, that's just it, it's not at all sure we'll get married."

Accustomed to heartbreak, Victoria clasps her hands together.

"Oh no, she's already married, and you're her lover!"

"Listen," Philippe protests, "don't complicate things. She's not married, but she doesn't want to leave her town for Paris, plus . . . we've sort of lost touch for a little while. With this tour we can't see each other very much . . . and she's really busy too."

"That's understandable," Victoria slips in. "A bookstore is a lot of work."

Choking on his cherry, he looks at his mother.

"So, you too? That's great, I . . ."

The order for silence is so startling that Philippe stifles his complaint.

"So why don't you move to her town?"

You're tough today, Victoria.

Philippe kicks the wall, catches the casserole that falls off the hook, and starts yelling:

"Because I have my work here, my house, my friends, and . . . and you."

Victoria doesn't flinch.

"I can move around, you know," she says. "I'm not paralyzed. I've had it up to here with Courbevoie and my public housing apartment."

Almost out of breath, he interrupts:

"Yeah, sure, it's easy to say that . . ."

"Don't try to make me an excuse for not going to this bookstore."

Crackers—my mother is completely crackers. She thinks she's going to sleep amidst the books and read for free for the rest of her life.

"You don't understand. What about my work? It no doubt seems secondary to you, too—"

Relentless, Victoria Lipinchky plants her fork in the carbonized meat.

"And her work? Doesn't that count? Don't you think books are more important than rolling on the floor and always losing?"

She'll never let me forget it.

It sounds good, books, sounds serious. It's "culture." Me, I'm the circus, the huge biceps and the tiny brain. Deep down, she's a pure bourgeoise. I can see her now talking with Jacqueline—*patati, patata*—oohing and aahing in front of big, vulgar Philippe. I've had it. I wish everyone would leave me alone and stop talking about it. My paints, a dozen cheeses, and I'm happy. I need absolutely nothing else . . . so just shove it . . .

Very slowly Philippe gets up, scratches his head, and sits back down under his mother's high-tension glare. He gathers his courage and feebly attempts to articulate his innermost feeling:

"Oh, I . . . I don't know."

chapter twenty-five

TUESDAY, the twelfth. One thirty P.M. Pantin wrestling ring.

The telephone rings in the gymnasium. Dripping with sweat, Léon Cro-Magnon wipes his palms on his tights and picks up the receiver, holding it like a frog between his thumb and index finger.

At the other end of the room Philippe Lipinchky is practicing some perilous leaps, causing the entire ring to vibrate.

"Philippe!"

The voice barely makes it through the racket of the punching balls. With his forearm Philippe wipes the sweat from between his eyebrows and makes a cone with his hand.

"What?"

Cro-Magnon bellows from the other end.

There is no noisier place in the world than a training room.

"Shut up a minute, damn it!" Philippe yells.

A featherweight flies by, bounces once on the mat, and shoots for the ceiling like a rocket.

"What did you say?"

Cro-Magnon approaches, grabs Philippe's fist, and sends him flying, only to fall back down like scrambled eggs. Léon follows and blocks his hold.

Philippe pivots, crosses his legs, shifts his lower back, and lifts his pal's 210 pounds.

"What did you wanna tell me?"

Léon rolls over Mephisto King's shoulders.

"We leave Saturday. We're gonna do Béziers, Narbonne, and Perpignan with the girls."

Philippe and his heavy load drop into a pile on the mat.

Cro-Magnon rubs his thigh.

"It'd be nice if you'd let me know next time you're gonna give up like that."

Philippe stares into space.

No news for twelve days. What is happening? It must be this deal with Fernande and Mauricette she can't take. It'll be a real circus at Perpignan. I'll have to invite the whole family or they'll never forgive me.

"Got problems?"

"You kiddin!? Things couldn't be better."

Léon shrugs his shoulders. Doesn't look that way. I've said it for years: as soon as there's a dame in a guy's life, everything goes whacko. The proof: It takes thirty tons to throw this guy, and just now with the force of a flea, he collapses like a dish rag. And the worst is that there's nothing I can do for him.

Wednesday, the thirteenth. Six thirty P.M. Courbevoie.

Victoria picks up the phone. She's a little surprised; usually he only calls every other day. So
since he called yesterday, now I know there's news
before he even says a word. Good or bad I don't
know, but I'll be able to tell from his voice. Not by
what he says, since he does his best not to tell me
things, just like his father. I didn't find out for three
weeks when he had bronchitis.

"Hello?"

"Hello, Maman."

He's got problems. Not too serious, but something's definitely wrong. If it was serious, he'd have
his overjoyous tone and then I'd know something's
fishy. Now he's going on and on . . . in a minute,
when he's run out of imagination, he'll say, "Oh
yeah, by the way, I forgot to tell you . . ." and
then I'll find out why he called.

"Oh yeah, by the way, I forgot to tell you, I won't
be there Sunday. We're going on tour."

"Ah, ah!"

Silence. This tour seems to complicate his existence.

"Are you going alone?"

"No, no, with Léon of course, and our partners."

"Your feminine partners?"

"Yeah, that's right, our usual partners."

"And where are you going?"

"Oh, a couple of towns, Béziers . . ."

He says a couple of towns, then "Béziers"—I've
brought a mental zero into the world.

"Béziers and where else?"

"Perpignan, yeah, I'm also going to Perpignan, if
you really wanna know."

Perpignan. So that's it. I knew something was

strange here. Hah! Don't think you can fool your old mother . . . Perpignan, that's where *she* lives, he told me last Sunday. Play innocent.

"Well, that's wonderful. Perpignan, that's where . . . what did you say her name was again?"

"Jacqueline."

"That's right, Jacqueline. That's really lucky, you can see each other."

He groaned. I'm sure of it, he groaned. Something's wrong here, no doubt about it.

"Aren't you happy?"

"Thrilled, I'm just thrilled."

Miserable. I can tell, he's miserable.

"I've got to go now, there're people waiting. Take care of yourself. I'll call you when I get back. It's a four-day trip."

"Have fun, dear, and . . ."

Click.

Something is really wrong and I know it is. This woman is jealous—jealous because he's wrestling with other women.

Someone's got to work this out, because I know Philippe: very sweet, but incapable of talking to a woman. Roll around on the ground, paint flowers, cook a leg of lamb, you name it, but get himself out of this one—I don't think so. There's only one person who can work this out and that's Victoria Lipinchky.

Anyway, I've got to meet her sooner or later. I'll tell her about Philippe . . . that she couldn't do better than. . . . I must calm down now. But I owe this to Philippe. If I could just work out his love life, I think I'd feel less remorse. I wouldn't have given you a pretty face, but I would have brought you together with a woman who doesn't find you so ugly. What a worry children are! You think you're finished when they're twenty; well, he's thirty-seven and look where I am! Plus I want to get to know her, and I have a reduction on the train. Plus they say the countryside is beautiful, plus, well, why not?

I'm going.

Friday, the fifteenth. Five o'clock. Collioure.

A beach, off-season, is about the deadest place you can find.

In midsummer, on these rocks, down these paths, along these ramparts, I used to imagine intense, joyous, teen-age loves.

Now, in the icy dawn of springtime, I can almost see the ghosts of kisses never received gliding past the café windows.

Suddenly I wanted to see this sea again . . . it's so close by car. So I stuck the keys under the door, took Fabienne under my arm, and here we are in a deserted café watching the wintry sea.

She smiles in the fog of her café-crème. Her eye-shadow is the same color as her raspberry-cyclamen wool scarf . . . splendid, but now I don't even care about the contrast we offer.

"I'm not the kind of girl who knows a man, Mademoiselle Puisset. They all forget about me in no time. They promise a lot, but they never keep those promises. Not that they're liars, I think they're very sincere; it's just that their sincerities don't last very long. There was one who wanted to take me to Argentina. I'm positive he was sure he wanted to do it when he proposed it, but when I arrived with my suitcase, he was just as sure he didn't. That's all there was to it."

Fabienne, who never says a word.

Today she's telling me about her unhappy loves while I'm trying to think how I'm going to tell Philippe about the baby, trying to decide if I should do it . . . and at the same time, I daydream, fantasizing about my flirtatious youth . . . rendezvous behind the towers, Mediterranean twilights, soft sandy finger tips on my golden arms of July.

Fabienne is staring at me. "You love this area, don't you?"

"I came here every year for vacation. We lived up high in the town. Maman said the air was fresher there."

Every year I lived different loves . . . the boy I saw in the bakery, a boy who went from one girl to the next: with him it was idyllic, feverish. All the places I explored alone, he was with me: on the jetty, in the waves, through the dark streets at night. All those years there was more romance in the imagination of that ugly little walleyed girl who read three books a day, shut up in her room, than in all the rest of the town.

Fabienne is laughing.

And here I am again after all these years . . . no more beautiful, a little more confident, and a baby on the way. It's about time!

Still, I had often decided to live alone, in the sorrow of my eighteen-year-old catastrophe. I swore to myself I wanted it, this sterility that befell me anyway. I went on and on about how good it was, not to have that child that no one wanted to give me.

Then . . . pow! Philippe.

It's not all that logical that an ugly woman fall in love with an ugly man. I have to admit, though, it's partly because he's ugly that I love him, which is ridiculous. It's more complicated than that, and simpler too. It happened, and that's that. For thirty years I dreamt of Gary Cooper and along came Lipinchky.

"I'm not too talkative, am I?"

"I'm the one who's talking too much," Fabienne says. "I'm bothering you with my troubles and you're so well-adjusted, your life is so calm."

"It's true," I say, "never the slightest adventure."

Somewhat disconcerted, Fabienne looks at her boss.

"Why are you laughing?"

Jacqueline Puisset plants her elbows on the table and leans toward her salesgirl.

"What's my name, Fabienne?"

"Jacqueline Puisset," she mumbles.

"Right. My residence and profession?"

She bats her long eyelashes, flustered.

"Bookseller in Perpignan, fifteen rue—"

Jacqueline lifts an imperative hand, halting the words on Fabienne's lips. She takes a deep breath and says:

"Well, sweet one, you should know that Jacqueline Puisset, bookseller in Perpignan, has, for three months, been the mistress of a bloodthirsty brute and now finds herself pregnant to the tips of her fingernails."

Noise of waves sifting through pebbles.

"No," Fabienne says.

"Yes," Jacqueline says.

Behind them, the percolator whistles in admiration.

The young girl's eyes round out. She murmurs very softly:

"A bloodthirsty brute?"

"Yes."

"Pregnant?"

"Yes."

Fabienne leans back, arms wide.

"That's wonderful!"

The salesgirl's perfumed cheek is soft against Jacqueline's lips. To think there was a time when I was always scolding her!

"If only that could happen to me," Fabienne exclaims, "but he's really too shy . . ."

"Are you Mademoiselle Puisset? There's a telephone call for you."

Only Noëlle knows I'm here.

"Jacqueline, it's Noëlle."

"What is it?"

"Guess."

"Did I call you or did you call me?"

"Always in a great mood. Isn't it doing you any good, your afternoon at the beach? I'll give you the news in three words: Philippe is coming. He tried to get hold of you at the store."

Philippe is coming. I feel myself turning green—green and fragile, like a lily pad.

"Now you can talk it all over."

I haven't told him anything, and I won't tell him anything until he suggests we get married. I will not use this kid to drag him to the justice of the peace. I'm happy, though, he's making the first move—it's better this way.

"He has a match on Saturday. I haven't told André yet, he won't be able to sleep . . ."

Cold shower. Through the café windows she watches the waves recede, inhaled by the horizon, and all that's left in the universe is a gray plain dotted with decaying seaweed. It's not because of me that he's coming. . . . Plus he's got the nerve to bring his whole circus with him—his leopard mistresses. Just wait, buddy, if you think you can parade around with your tigresses in front of me . . . I'll just have to set up my own show. I can fight too, you know. Arduous males aren't so hard to come by.

Jacqueline walks out onto the boardwalk and heads for the waves at a hectic pace. Fabienne gets up and follows. Something is wrong here.

Friday, the fifteenth. Eleven P.M. Perpignan.

I can't sleep.

Tomorrow we're going to the match. Papa didn't want to, but they gave us the tickets, so we have to go. I saw the posters for it. He's fighting against lady panthers. It's written real big. It's gonna be swell. I can't go to sleep. Tata's coming too, 'cause it's her friend. We're all going. It's a good thing it's on Saturday, 'cause that way the next day's Sunday, and if it was a day when the next day wasn't Sunday, I couldn't go, 'cause it's only good on Saturday 'causa school.

I can't sleep. It's always like that when I'm going to a match.

*   *   *

Friday, same time. Perpignan.

She just doesn't realize.

It's understandable though, and maybe it's better that way. Sometimes she seems overjoyed, then the next minute she's furious, and now this idea to go there with a man! Of course, I can see why she's so confused. If I were her, I'd already be knitting the booties. But we're so different. . . . She must be afraid, underneath that courageous shell; but still, it's so wonderful that it's happened to her. I would never have believed it—I'd given up. I wanted so much for her to know a man, I did everything I could . . . and now, a man and a child! Still, she must have tried to strangle me a hundred times, once with my first pair of stockings, just like in murder mysteries. Later on, though, she calmed down. "Madame" said she'd really rather read than go out, but it wasn't true. I know she wasn't happy very often, maybe never before meeting this Philippe. . . .

It really shook me up when I found out. A baby! Jacqueline! I'll be an aunt—that'll seem strange. I'll have to help her with the doctor and the papers and everything; she'll be totally lost. What frightens me is the way people are going to react. There'll be more than a little gossip . . . I wonder how it'll affect her business. Anyway, that's not the most important thing. I'll help her out at first, with the bottles, the diapers and all—she'll be overwhelmed. Plus, at her age . . .

I can't get to sleep, and I'm sure for her it's even worse. If she doesn't say something tomorrow night, I'm going to have a talk with this wrestler myself.

I thought she stayed in Paris an awfully long time

for that convention. That girl; the day she tells me a secret or two . . . I wonder how it'll all work out. Nothing's ever simple with her, but this time she takes the cake!

Saturday, 11:30 A.M. Perpignan.
Place de la Loge. It's nice to sit and have a drink in the Middle Ages. In the ancient square squeezed between sculptured stone houses, the aroma of *pastis* drifts through thirteenth-century arcades. The ice cubes clinking in the glasses reflect flamboyant Gothic windows. Fabienne sighs, fishing mechanically for the curly lemon peel in her martini. She takes it and crushes it in her porcelain teeth. Her immense eyes devour her companion, who has yet to touch his Dubonnet. He concludes:

> *With a quiet sigh, a languid shiver,*
> *The wounded nymph died at the banks of the*
> *river.*

Silence.
The stunning salesgirl awakens from a long sleep of ecstasy.
"It's so beautiful!" she sighs.
With a last dramatic hand gesture, Trotsky knocks the plate of olives off the table, turns purple, and admits:
"I had no idea that you would like this sort of . . ."
"Why, Monsieur Javier?"
Such sweetness in her voice (the exquisite pallor of your words, my loved one!). Trotsky feels his heart pounding. This is too extraordinary, too per-

fect, too surprising, too marvelous . . . my God, if my students passed by now and saw me with this ravishing young girl!!

"Mademoiselle Fabienne, I don't know how to express to you . . ."

He stops. If only she were Marceline Desbordes Valmore plus Nadine de Hautepin plus Rosemonde Gérard plus Anne de Noailles plus . . . My God, how can I make her understand the kind of emotion surging through my being?

"Monsieur Javier, I have some free tickets that came to the bookstore this morning, and I was wondering if you'd mind accompanying me?"

My prayers have been answered! Tonight I'll be with her. Life goes so fast—we're living at two thousand miles per hour. Well, so be it—let's accept this wild rhythm.

Trotsky makes a violent gesture with his head and feels his soul inflate, fling out the banners, and soar to the upper vaults of the enormous arcade. He announces:

"Not at all, Mademoiselle Fabienne. I'd be more than happy to."

Fabienne bats her eyelashes. In this instant she's the most beautiful girl in the world.

"It's for a wrestling match," she says angelically.

Trotsky, who with a profound aversion to all sports has never in his life held a badminton racquet longer than three minutes, wiggles under the narrow shoulders of his velvet jacket.

"Wonderful," he says, "I love it."

They look at each other. Around them the square is playing at looking like Venice, as the old bachelor

watches the mists of the Adriatic dissipate in Fabienne's eyes.

Saturday, 3:30. Perpignan.
Anselme Bertouin yawns, grabs the newspaper,
glances vaguely at the crossword puzzle, throws it
down feebly, and walks toward the TV.
He turns on the TV, watches the news commenta-
tor's face come into view, then turns it off again. The
worst, he thinks, is that I'm not even an alcoholic.
What's more, by a stroke of exceptionally bad luck,
he had no dossiers to bring home this weekend: he's
too conscientious, he's ahead on his deadlines, he's
completely on top of his work. His boss is happy
with him and there's nothing left to do but accept
the boredom . . .
Anselme wanders pointlessly into the bathroom.
The paint is beginning to chip.
I am *not* going to take another shower.
The small room is coated in a glowing lima bean
green, an aquatic color, which in the light shades
his complexion.
He looks at himself in the mirror and wonders if
the only reason he'd been able to live with his face
was that he'd always considered it temporary. It
was quite strange, this impression he had that beauty
would come to him some day, one day, sometime
later. . . . Tomorrow I'll be someone else . . .
Anselme picks up his nail clippers. The ivory
moons bounce in the porcelain. I'm not ugly. It's
just that people don't see me, that's all. It's as simple
as that.
I'm thirsty.

Tomorrow's Sunday. In the afternoon I'll have some sherry in a mustard glass. I brought the bottle up in my attache case, between two dossiers, so the concierge wouldn't gossip. It's my little treat, my "*gourmandise.*"

She's incredible, the concierge.

"Frankly, Monsieur Bertouin, do I look my age?"

"No, Madame Espérandieu."

"Monsieur Bertouin tells everyone I don't look my age."

I liked Sundays before—the streets were different then. I'd go down, all excited, to the downtown neighborhoods, squeezing in my hot little hand my money for the movies, a Mickey Mouse comic book, a popsicle. I liked climbing back up the terraces where men were laughing over their cocktails, surrounded by geraniums. I was a child then.

I wasn't born around here. Maybe that's why I don't know anyone and they call me "the doormat." I'm a joke, probably because I'm always a little bit afraid. The worst is that I don't know exactly what of—it's vague, wavering somewhere between the pit of my stomach and the edge of the universe.

I've never bought a datebook—it's pointless, I never have any rendezvous. I never get invited anywhere, or maybe just once, never twice; people see right off I'm no live wire. I've always had the impression that the party starts just as I shut the door behind me. I don't know exactly why. I'm not ugly, nor particularly stupid, I think, but my life is gloomy, my days have no sparkle.

I could shave again, but for whom? Well, it is a little stubby under the jawbone . . .

Anselme puts down his clippers and examines his gray eyes: a dull expanse, a flat landscape to delve into . . .

You add it all up: average schoolwork; episodic, feeble romances; a nonstop job; and my days in front of me to be filled like an accountant's book, a life of identical days lined up one after the other, a life like an addition column.

I wonder why I had the phone installed.

That blade was too old, I couldn't have hoped for much.

A few girls' faces at the doors of the high school, a twelve-year-old neighbor when I was eight, and then Suzanne to top it off—romantically speaking, not a thrilling existence. Still, we *were* engaged for six years. I can't say I really suffered that much when she went out of my life; in fact I wonder if she was ever really in it.

There's no question, I'm not ugly; there's even something sort of charming around the nose, at least it seems to me there is. But I'm so blah, that's my problem.

And the result: Saturday afternoon in Perpignan spent staring into the bathroom mirror, working out the nonexistent balance sheet of my life. Time passes and at the end is death.

Death for a man whom no one remembered even when he was living. Death is ridiculous really, when you've never been particularly alive. Never any mail, and this Bakelite block of silence they call the telephone, which never rings. Death can come from anywhere; it could spring up from this new blade: a rectangle with no thickness, ordinary, unimposing; death in proportion to the man, as negligible as a safety razor.

Suzanne never sent me any news. I still have her disconnected number. Death in a bathroom, Saturday afternoon in Perpignan. A little shot of aperitif to give me courage. Maybe I'll get a few lines in the local newspaper. I'll bet anything they get my name wrong; it seems easy to remember, but I'm always amazed at the ways people deform it.

I'm not going to start crying . . . it must be the steam, or else it's because I'm just too lonely. . . . It won't hurt—a stinging line—then it'll go gently, just like draining the oil from a car . . .

Whether it's their fault or mine or both I don't know, but this town has let me down. I wasn't made for this blasting sun, or rugby, or the bullfights . . . tough luck for me.

A last bet: If someone comes or if the telephone rings, I'll try again. If someone calls me, no matter who it is—my boss, the tax collector, anyone—I'll stay alive, I'll call Suzanne, I'll give it another go. I'll give myself until four o'clock, that's ten minutes . . . but no one will come, no one will call, there's no risk there.

Anselme Bertouin is still staring at himself. The sky is blue and clear as a diamond. On the smooth porcelain the water flows silently, silky and patient. No sound can be heard. Anselme shuts his eyes. Ten minutes.

Saturday, 3:54 P.M. Perpignan.

Jacqueline hangs up hard enough to crack the telephone. She looks up. Before her stands a little old lady in a fruit-trimmed hat. She almost succeeds in resembling a Russian empress.

A smile suddenly illuminates the wrinkled face, and the dignified grandmother extends an open hand toward Jacqueline.

"I'm Victoria Lipinchky," she says.

Saturday, 8:28 P.M. Perpignan.

The lights in the gymnasium are about to dim. The audience takes its pose. It's the moment when bodies are getting as comfortable as possible in the hollow of the seats. Clouds of smoke float by at head level, thickest in the rectangular cube of light awaiting the combat. The neon lights hidden in the beams spread a vague, sickly lima bean tint over the first fifteen rows. Full house tonight: from the ring, spreading back to the farthest corners.

Opposite the officials, we see, in a green dress, Noëlle Louberan; in checkered socks, her son André. Licorice bag in hand, he chomps frenetically, eyes glued on the entrance tunnel. On his left, a tense Jacqueline Puisset seems to have swallowed a bag of unpinned grenades. At her side, Anselme Bertouin, stiff and pallid. His neighbor is swinging her feet back and forth; on her lap is a hat whose cherries she is violently fingering. It's Victoria Lipinchky.

Behind her: Fabienne. She is listening in veneration to her neighbor, who for the first time in his life has parted his hair on the side and no longer looks so much like Trotsky. They have yet to make any declarations—perhaps they never will.

Everyone is there.

They are waiting for the curtain to rise for the last act.

Jacqueline feels it in her bones that it'll all be settled here, tonight. It was around a similar ring that it all started and it's here it'll all finish. She can feel it to the tips of her fingernails. Maybe everyone feels it, which would explain the almost respectful silence in the hall. As the lights dim and the cymbals and gongs reverberate, the loudspeaker announces the big match the way the heralds announced the arrival of soldiers and demigods at the gates of ancient cities:

"And now, a *grrr*eat match in two rounds with a possible run-off between . . ."

The spotlights zero in on bouncing purple legs as the ladies climb through the ropes, the racket at deafening decibels. Their manes are flowing. Jacqueline crosses her arms and grits her teeth.

"And the already famous terrifying duo, I mean Cro-Magnon Man and . . ."

Mephisto King twists around, scarlet cape soaring, unfurling back onto his massive shoulders.

"Go get 'em!" André yells.

The horror mask turns toward the kid and the colossal's fingers salute. André digs his elbow into the maternal ribs.

"D'you see? He saw me!"

Victoria punches her hat. If he doesn't win tonight he's going to hear from me—the one time I come, he could at least make an effort.

Philippe grabs the ropes and shakes them to check the give.

She came with some kind of goon who looks like

he takes himself for the grand duke of Perpignan. Luckily Maman told me; it would have been quite a shock. And then, the telephone call with her distant princess voice: "I'll be coming with a friend, but we can talk tomorrow."

Cro-Magnon crouches in the corner, his flint skull shining like a mirror.

"Not in great shape tonight, Toto, I can see it right through the mask."

This is ridiculous, I have a ridiculous profession. And those two over there, wouldn't they be better off taking care of their kids or fixing dinner or something, rather than joining in on this circus act?

"We're clowns, Léon, real clowns. Me, I'm the devil, and you, you're the caveman. It's a puppet show; we've never grown up."

"Round one."

"I repeat," Léon says, "you are not in great shape."

Here we go. . . . The hall explodes; Fernande takes the first hold and Léon gets thrown. Of course she's had it with me and this wrestling bit—it's not a profession that inspires confidence, not like her nice little friend there. She told me his name, but I can't remember it. . . . He must work in an office, that guy. I'm sure he's never been disguised in his entire life. He's probably got some act, but surely not as exhibitionist as mine.

This certainly is my big night—Maman and everything. Hopefully she won't climb up on the ring and bawl me out.

"Hey, Mephisto, you twiddlin' your thumbs?"

A voice from one of the last rows. Some real

jokesters here in Perpignan. I feel like breaking
something and I can't even take it out on my adversary. It's not poor Mauricette's fault.

Léon flies across the ring, followed by the referee's piercing whistle; he lands willy-nilly and tags
his pal.

On with the music.

Accompanied by wild screams, jeers, and whistles, Philippe comes forth.

Here I am, Anselme Bertouin, at a wrestling
match, and Suzanne's going to call next week.

The loudest telephone ring I've ever heard in my
life! It rattled my teeth, that *bbrrring*. In the best-
sellers that's what they call a miracle.

"Hello, Monsieur Bertrandieu?"

Didn't matter, I'm used to it. I even said it was
me anyway, I wanted so much for it not to be a
mistake . . .

Puisset . . . didn't ring any bells. Then I remembered, the dynamic bookseller with the weird eye
at Louberan's, a colleague's sister-in-law—it was
good enough for me. Now I'm sitting next to her;
she fascinates me, this woman who has no idea she
saved my life.

I don't really know why I'm here, in fact; before
I could bat an eyelash, she'd whisked me off to this
wrestling gala. God knows why. Suzanne's coming
Friday—she may be more a part of my life than I
ever thought possible. Color has come back . . . in
this hall, in the streets, everywhere. . . . I owe it all
to her.

Anselme leans over.

"Thank you, mademoiselle."

Jacqueline jumps in her seat and looks at him.

"For what?"

"It's complicated," Anselme smiles. "I'll tell you about it one day. I owe you a lot."

"Not at all," Jacqueline says. "First of all, the tickets weren't expensive and, well, it's my pleasure."

"No, you don't understand . . . I'm getting married soon."

"Congratulations," Jacqueline groans.

Another hopeful off the list.

I have never in my life felt so walleyed. It was ridiculous to come here with this Bertoudieu—just childish, a jealous woman's reaction. So Philippe works with two women? What of it? If he worked in an office I wouldn't give him a hard time because there were two typists in the next room, and anyway . . .

Vrrroom!

The two colossals run straight into each other and collapse. The ladies start a war dance around the heap of worn-out muscles. The referee counts.

Victoria Lipinchky jumps up.

"Will you get up!"

André's eyes fill with tears.

Noëlle shakes her head.

Fabienne burns the thousand fires of her beauty, leaning her ear toward Trotsky, who finishes in a whisper:

"And Eden closed its gates on the birdsong . . ."

"Nine . . . and ten!"

The referee slices the air with his arms. The vanquished brutes go back to their corners.

"Wanda and Tania, winners of the first round by a knockout."

Sighing with disappointment, Victoria sits back down.

"I always said he was a good-for-nothing."

Jacqueline's hand rests on the old woman's arm. The two women look at each other.

They never stopped chattering during the whole round. I saw them. I could do four perilous double leaps in a row and they wouldn't even notice. It was *patati, patata*. With their heads almost touching. This guy irritates me beyond belief, puffing out his chest every two minutes. It's strange she never told me about him. . . .

At the other end of the ring Mauricette wipes her arms with a towel and stretches the small of her back.

"When you do the armholes, block it first and press with a damp cloth so that you don't have little gaps or pockets."

Legs straight, Fernande presses her nose to her knee to loosen the deltoids, then does a couple of jumps in place to keep her going.

"Round two."

Anyway, I couldn't care less; I was a lot better off before: my watercolors, my quiet little feasts in my flat, vacations in the sun—Tunisia or elsewhere. There's no reason to load myself down with a woman, a bookseller, the whole bit. . . . Keep it cool, Toto, you're not twenty years old, about to jump out the window over this.

Fernande blocks Mephisto's fist and lands a forearm chop, but she doesn't hold back enough and hits his nose. Philippe sprawls backwards, eyes filled with tears. Fernande plunges and takes him down, his head at the edge of the ring.

Anselme Bertouin, two yards from the wrestler, leans toward his savior:

"In fact, it's always sort of the same with these shows, isn't it?" he asks. "When it's not one who falls, it's the other one."

He's babbling on and on to her. He looks less like a potato than I do, but more like a leek with no leaves. Culture, that's the difference; we're both ugly, but me, I've got it in the biceps, and him, he's got a lot less than he thinks upstairs, I'm sure of that. He must have won her over with some spiel, probably drags her around museums and ciné-clubs. On their honeymoon they'll gape at beautiful paintings. I can hear him now, that little ass: "Come see the Rubens—what do you think of this Rembrandt, chérie?" Deadly.

At this precise moment, Philippe Lipinchky makes his decision.

I know it's a stupid one, but I've never been too intelligent, and it's the only one I can come up with. This guy drives me crazy, I can't take it, I know he's making fun of me.

The ceiling spins, he pulls himself loose, tossing aside his torturer, and shoots out like a hundred-meter Olympic champion. His feet leave the ground.

An angel leap.

Crying out, wings of fury: vengeance pursues the crime. The death dive.

Philippe cuts an arc through the air, and realizes that it's because his suffering has never been so vivid or so real that he's resorted to this ridiculous burlesque; as though overwhelmed by an unbearable pain, his only refuge is in somersaults and slapstick, like the clowns in the theater who are never so funny as when Colombine escapes with Arlequin. . . .

Sad Arlequin in his joyless costume, poor plain Colombine, and me, fat Paillasse, a wounded soul crashing through the air in an idiotic leap of desperation.

The sound of cracking chairs echoes through the gymnasium. Jaw dropped in bewilderment, Cro-Magnon contemplates the spectacle: Mephisto King has just crushed some unlucky guy who is wiggling desperately under the massive wrestler.

Jacqueline is no less stupefied. Victoria tears the last grapes from the vine in one handful.

The bookseller stares at the demonic mask and bellows through the racket:

"You could have killed him! You did it on purpose!"

Philippe stares at the ground. Up above, the referee is counting.

"I know it was stupid, but I couldn't resist."

I won. I've more than won. I've made you furious, my big tough guy. It was all a joke. I want to tell you I love you, that I love only you. Who else would I, who'd never loved, love? I don't know what I'm saying . . .

Here they are all around me, except Leekhead, who's underneath me and probably getting a little tired of it. Even Léon's here, and the girls, Fabienne, Noëlle, André, Mimosa Man, and Maman, who's no doubt gonna let me have it . . .

"Well, you lost again," she says. "Hurry up, you can't just lie around all night."

"Yes I can."

"What?"

Philippe takes off his mask and smiles his excuses to the assembly.

"My leg is broken."

epilogue

"Jacqueline."

The bookseller turns around, her hand resting on the doorknob.

Visiting hours have been over for forty-five minutes. My knees are trembling. A normal reaction. My room was right across the hall. When he makes that dopey face it reminds me of a cartoon I saw with André at the Splendid last week.

"What'll we name it?"

The rest of my days on the mattress of your pectorals, my big wrestler. . . . We've talked about it all, I've got to go, and now, with that Walt Disney bear face, you ask me these questions that fill me with tears . . .

Philippe caresses the hair tickling his chin. Now there's this kid squeezed between our bellies, the child of the woman who broke my right femur and almost my heart.

The child of the convention, Paris's child, the

child of the three days when I was beautiful, with my super jeans, my fantastic clogs; when I was twenty years old for the first time.

"You have an idea?"

Philippe loosens his hug and looks at her.

"Go ahead, let's hear yours."

"Marc," Jacqueline says. "And yours?"

Philippe grimaces.

"Denise," he says.

Jacqueline's lips rest briefly on the wrestler's cheek.

"So, we agree on everything," she says. "Why are you laughing?"

"You're laughing too."

"Why?"

Jacqueline Puisset turns toward the door. She'll be back tomorrow. The room reeks of mimosas: Trotsky and Fabienne brought them together. Things follow their natural course. It looks like those two will win their match; and me, I've just won mine. On the chair is Victoria's forgotten hat with one last leaf shining. She's won too.

"Tell me, why are you laughing?"

Jacqueline opens the door and flings out her arms. Yes, there's no question I've won. Outside, the city climbs into its bed. Clear skies throughout the area.

"Because we're beautiful," she says.